Contents

POETRY

TRANSLATION FOLIOS

On the Cover / Stephanie Syjuco
Total Transparency Filter (Portrait of N), 2017
Archival pigment inkjet
40" x 30"

KATIE CONDON

Book Blurb in the American Style

A caveman discovered the power of his dick
& pressed it into one woman & then another, eventually creating
the world's most important poet since the fall of the Roman Empire:
Katie Condon! Antiquity, antiquity! She sings of afterbirth & blood!
Today, the snarkiest poet since the discovery of fire invites you
to her home for a soy chai latte on the lawn! Thereafter,
she will take you on a tour of her three-bedroom ranch:
in the living room hangs Sappho's portrait as a reminder
of whom she has surpassed with her wiles! Talk
of *Dream Songs*! Here, friends, nothing is boring!
The most critical poet since the Big Bang invites you
into her bathroom where the seashell soaps smell of Coleridge,
of a mariner's sweet-boozed breath, of sunshine, and brine!
Her bedroom, where Katie Condon sleeps & fucks & drools, is bright;
dust filtering through sunlight like the stars in her irises.

All Light Ends

I feel my daughter move for the first time
at a cocktail party. I am stuck in conversation
with one of those people who pontificates
about anything to anyone they can corner—this guy
going on about Rumi with a bacon-wrapped date
half-chewed in the corner of his mouth.
The wound is the place light enters you, he says
Rumi said and that's when I feel her
assert her body in a little flail, responding,
The wound begins in the womb, where all light ends.
Absurd of me to think she hadn't been
listening from the beginning. Our companion
has moved on to a miniature quiche and Lacan's
lack. Barely noticeable through the window,
evening tints the party briefly crimson.
My loneliness was never my own.

ANDREW COLLARD

Loneliness in the Key of Sprawl

I do the pigeon, when the chorus hits,
              along a sidewalk
        modeling the strange shapes

weather breaks us into, I do the jogger
                and the rhododendron,
        though I know you are, by this hour,

far away. There was a house here, or
              there could've been,
        the space hushed as an instrumental

passage in the measure of a street
                wracked with expansion.
        Somewhere, the water backing up

through a storm drain floods a corridor
                at rush hour, seeping
        into the cabins of stranded cars,

and the rhythms that have carried us
              from lot to lot
        these last months are swallowed.

I do the evergreen, though today it seems
              I have no place
        in history, I do the earwig

and the cul-de-sac, but I receive no indication
              of response. Before *origin*,
        before memory and the thought

of home, there are questions that go on
                without me, the banality
        of someone deciding what to eat,

and with who. Consider how precariously
                we could live together:
        you, in the bedroom above, and me,

always distracted with the idea
                of coming up. We could
        learn, at last, the dryer vent

and the elusive junk mail, we could scare
                the neighbors all week long
        inventing new, unmanageable steps

as the daylilies stashed behind the garage
                explode through a season's worth
        of grasping vines and branches.

JOSEPH J. CAPISTA

Celestial Navigation Made Easy

Some days the wind doesn't want your caution.

Some days God comes like night in the thief.

Some days when I see a woman with a cigarette in one hand and a baby in the other hand I think to myself, "I really want cigarette."

Some days you retrofit your dreams to suit your very life.

Some days you see so clearly Patty Kirkman's Elvis staring down at you, that poster of him in his pinwheel jumpsuit framed above her pea green Hotpoint.

Some days questions of high art and low art are resolved by asking yourself whether you'd prefer that piece embroidered on your socks.

Some days macerating strawberries in the bowl resemble no one's heart, some days Romans flossed songbirds from between their teeth, some days, nail by nail, you dismantle the firmament.

Some days you light a votive for St. Francis Picabia, then pray his intercession may help you enter what others deem heaven.

Picabia who, as a boy, copied five Spanish paintings from his grandfather's collection, reframed and rehung each imitation, then peddled the originals for rare postage stamps. *Philately*: "loving" + "exemption from a payment."

Some days protecting your child from the world means protecting them from you.

Some days life's grammar is love. Mostly, though, it's time. Mostly, I have learned that I am bad at others.

All we ever have, I tell errant bees, is all we ever have.

Sometimes the bridge is made of river.

Sometimes the night reveals exactly where you aren't. Look up: right sky ahead, wrong stars.

MYRONN HARDY

Easter

Offer lilies near the bed.
Open the blinds to be blinded
temporarily. Later lamb
with rosemary   waxy potatoes   red wine.

Who you were   over. Sunlight
through eyes   skin   as you
walk   as seagulls shred trash
bags   fight for chicken

femurs   fish fingers foul.
Women in church parking
lots wear white dresses. Hydrangeas
dangle from their palms. You don't

expect the giant rhododendron.
Its purple blossoms destroy.
Years ago   you stood
beneath it watching a firebird

pull away. Dust in your face as it
pulled away to disappear.
The way you crawled
home   the river

you made. You're
no longer a river.
Resurrected as skin   rhythm.
Walk with me?

JENNIFER MILITELLO

Nativity

A CHILD IS BORN OF straw and windfall and wool. A child is born of iron nails driven in. A door added. A door removed. A child is born of diving deep into the ocean. A child is born of the fibers from a strange bone grafted to the hand.

One comes in the middle of the night. One comes just after noon. One is born in the lazy days of July during a heat wave that leaves the new parents panting in their sleep. One is born on the first day of a new year, of a new decade, during a snow squall that blanks the walls of the understaffed hospital room with a whiteness that whittles all vision sharp like a knife.

One child breaks the amniotic sac three weeks early with a kick and leaves behind a placenta that has to be separately expelled. One child wedges its way lengthwise across the midsection in the last few days and then is born inside the sac, like an infant charmed or bewitched.

Mara's children were as different as their births. A daughter and a son. One with a tuft of slick black hair. One with eyes so blue they seemed clear.

Each time, Goat did not understand it was time. Mara said, *My water broke*, She said, *I'm having contractions*. He replied by asking, *Are you sure?*

A child is born of moss and melancholy and birdsong and an invasive species of grass. A child is born of the silence in a room. One child is born of pain. One child is born of strength. One child is born of measured breathing. One child is born of gripping the hospital bed handrails, of reading again and again the instructions for each button: *Push in case of an emergency. Push to raise head of bed. Push to lower the railing. Push for reading light. Push to call a nurse.*

Push. Push.

Mara's daughter was born in the middle of the day, and the exposure she felt during the birth reminded her of making well-lit love in the afternoon. Her son had been born in the dark, as a rendezvous, a secret, arrived in the night in a room kept dim, among the glowing sheets and a microwave clock, with Goat silent beside Mara, Goat who had chosen to stay alongside her head during the labor and then moved to cut the cord. Mara whispered, *We have a son.* Took her baby to hold him against her skin. She held him and would not let the nurses take him away to the room where babies were placed in anonymous bassinets when they wanted the mother to get some sleep. She was afraid he would cry without her, or that they would feed him from a bottle and he wouldn't learn to breastfeed, or that they would bring the wrong baby back.

A child is born of asking what will happen or what to expect again and again.

A child is born of refusing drugs and hearing the nurse scoff and say: Everyone says that, and in the end everyone wants drugs.

A child is born of the absence of a man urging her on, encouraging her, speaking to her softly. Of a man failing to reply when the nurse says, *Your wife is incredible. She never lost control. I'll be talking about this birth for a long time.*

A child is born of shouts that seem to come from a room down the hall but actually come from the throat. Of watching an abdomen ridge up and release like the back of an ancient sea animal cresting the waves, of a gap in the stomach muscles that will never repair, four inches across, into which the mother will be able to dip the fingertips of her hand.

Of the doctor saying to push. Of the doctor saying to stop. Of a doctor commanding a slight push then release, and a nurse whispering, *Such control.*

A child is born of a nurse finally saying, *She's here.*

LATER, WHEN THE children become allergic, Mara stops eating dairy and soy. She changes to a special supplemental formula that tastes like salt and that the children will not eat. She starts a diet that consists only of meat and potatoes and rice and loses weight quickly, fat at first, and then the muscle base she built when young that has always kept her fit. She loses her energy and sits on the couch in a robe each day nursing and holding the children upright while they sleep. Each a child who had started to cry at two weeks old, a raw form of crying, an inconsolable wail, and would not stop, a cry she asked the doctor about, with a different sound, until he tells her she has read too many books, and that the *range of pain* her baby is experiencing is normal.

She calls the doctor late when the child cries in the night, and when he returns the call she finally, after months of crying and months of calls, says she needs to see a specialist. The specialist drips liquid onto a smear of stool she's delivered on a sample card and the liquid turns blue. The child is bleeding from his colon because he is allergic to milk. The test has taken two seconds at most. She thinks of the doctor who has cost her child three months of pain, how at her last visit he had called the baby famous, as in "Oh look. It's the famous _____ here yet again."

It is a mother's job to keep the babies safe when a father cannot not see they are sick.

Mara is told the children also have acid reflux and cannot lie down flat. She tries every option, car seat, baby hammock, bouncy chair, crib wedge, and in the end none of them work, so she sleeps in a chair every night and holds each child upright in her arms because she cannot let her baby *cry it out* when that baby is in pain. She returns two sling-like carriers that are supposed to help but are later recalled when they are linked to several infant deaths. She feeds the children a horrible medicine with a dropper twice a day. She tries to taste the medicine and the taste is so bad that its memory even now burns into her tongue.

She eats nothing. She mixes a homemade formula of safflower oil and protein powder and rice milk. She tries to drive to the store or the mall though her children cry in the car. One child can scream nonstop all the way across three states. She goes to court when she is pulled over for speeding and desperately gestures toward her wailing child and the officer hands her a ticket anyway. She tells the judge about the allergies and reflux, provides documentation of each, talks of trying to soothe a baby while driving and of not being able to eat. She wins her case and does not have to pay the fine.

A father goes to work each morning. He comes home and functions each night.

As the children start to eat solid foods, Mara keeps dairy and soy from their diet. She reintroduces the offending foods every six months once they turn two, and when the pain begins again, she brings them in and their samples test positive for blood. Once, when the oldest child is almost three, she brings him to be tested and the usual doctor isn't there. The doctor she sees says to her, *So you are telling me we are going to test him because he's been fussy.* She says yes. She tries to sit up straighter as she explains what she had been through for the last three years. She remembers to keep it brief. She remembers to stay calm. She takes a deep breath. She says, I brought the card, you just have to put the liquid on it. The doctor says, *Fine, but when he is sixteen and fussy, I'm not going to test for an allergy,* and whisks out of the room. When the doctor returns, his body language has changed. He does not apologize. The mother sits very still as he tells her the sample tested positive for blood.

Once their teeth come in and they start on solids, she is afraid to feed the children. She isn't sure how small to cut the food or how much to let them shovel in or whether they can chew. She performs the Heimlich maneuver twice when they start choking, sweeps a finger across the empty mouths, compresses the abdomen until the food comes out, and is left trembling from the realization that she has saved her children's lives.

Mara feels relief at the normalcy when, at a year and a half old, one child falls against the cabinet corner and splits open his head and has to go to the hospital for stitches. When one child brings home lice from daycare and passes it to the whole family, she is glad the children do not feel pain. One child's belly button needs to be cauterized closed. She takes a child to the hospital for stitches. She picks the nits from the children's heads. A doctor takes the blue fishline stitches out in his office once the wound has healed and tapes them to a piece of gauze as a souvenir.

When Mara says she needs to rest, Goat says, then rest, but he never needs rest himself and he cannot understand her need. He says, then rest, but his voice says, why do you need rest, in the tone of it, underneath the words.

When the children begin to twitch and stutter and show sensitivities to the feel of water and clothing and light, she reads an article about arsenic in the rice milk they constantly drink and calls to have the children tested. In her office, the doctor says she has never tested a child for arsenic before though she's been a doctor for more than ten years. Mara stays calm and takes a deep breath and asks the doctor again to test them. When the results come back, the levels of arsenic in the children's urine is three times the amount that's safe. But the arsenic isn't in the rice milk. The arsenic is in the well.

She has been feeding her children arsenic. She has been drinking arsenic for seven years.

She sees the other mothers with their neatly dressed children who nap in their strollers, with their hair combed and their makeup on, running errands and marking things off on their lists. They look put together. They look fine. They don't have the wild look that she knows she must have. They aren't too thin. They don't have dark circles under their eyes. A father can be fine, but a mother kills herself to keep her children alive.

As the years pass, the children grow and function and heal. The daughter learns to throw a ball with accuracy and swim like a fish. The boy lazes through his days intelligently with a sensitivity to time and light. The girl plants a peach tree and picks raspberries and blueberries for jam while the boy leaves empty snack wrappers in his wake and does all the family's laundry to earn money to buy video games he wants. Slowly they begin to be able to lie down flat, slowly they begin to eat new foods, slowly they learn to sleep in their beds.

Goat goes to work. He cooks meals. Looks at Mara with eyes so blue they seem clear.

A mother is born of discomfort and the crush of folding clothes and doing dishes and the crush of soothing a crying child and holding a child's hand and doing what needs to be done. Mother like a mouse that has died under the heating vent, mother like the rabbit found headless in the car engine, mother like the ant colony poisoned and hidden somewhere in the wall. Washing away, bobbing downstream. Made of bones. Made of torso and hands and feet. A mother is offspring of the rocking and rocking and singing and feeding and holding, and a mother has died, and can she be reborn.

Translation Folio

VIVIAN LAMARQUE

Translator's Introduction

Geoffrey Brock

OVER THE PAST HALF CENTURY, Vivian Lamarque has carved out a singular space in the landscape of Italian poetry. Often bringing the gestures and rhythms of nursery rhymes and fairy tales to the childhood traumas and adult passions that give shape and meaning to her work, she has created a powerful body of poetry that is both highly personal and highly mythologized. She has published a dozen collections of poetry (along with many children's books and translations of modern French poetry) but only one—her second, *Il Signore d'oro*, translated by Pasquale Verdicchio as *The Golden Man* (Ekstasis Editions 2016)—has appeared in English. The poems presented here are from her beautiful and crucial first book, *Teresino*, which won Italy's prestigious Viareggio Prize for a first book and which laid the groundwork for everything that comes later. Her newest volume, *Amore da vecchia*, just won the Premio Strega, Italy's top poetry prize, and several other major awards.

Lamarque was born Vivian Daisy Donata Provera Pellegrinelli Comba on April 19, 1946, in Tesero, in the northern Italian province of Trento, to a Waldensian mother. Being illegitimate, she was given up for adoption, at the age of nine months, to a Catholic family from Milan. At the age of four, her adoptive father died. At the age of ten, she learned she had two mothers and wrote her first two poems: "The Good Lady M." and "The Bad Lady M." Since her adoption she has continued to live in Milan.

In the 1970s, she began publishing her work in leading Italian journals and attracting critical attention from several leading poets. In 1984, three years after debuting with *Teresino*, she began Jungian analysis, which inspired her next three books, all dedicated to her analyst. Since that trilogy she has published half a dozen new collections and, in 2002, a collected poems. She has also produced a large body of translations, both of "adult" literature (mostly French poetry) and of children's literature. By now she is widely considered, as Nicola Gardini wrote in the *Times Literary Supplement*, "one of Italy's most acclaimed and cherished poets."

Her childhood traumas—her adoption and her adoptive father's death—set in motion a lifelong exploration of origin, identity, and doubleness, weighty questions that she often explores with a deft and affecting lightness of touch. Both as a writer and a reader, I've long been interested in that quality that Italo Calvino, in *Six Memos for the Next Millennium*, calls *lightness* and in the ways it can, in the right hands, underwrite the heaviest of themes. Calvino quotes Paul Valéry (whom Lamarque has translated): "Il faut être léger comme l'oiseau, et non comme la plume"—"one must be light like the bird, not like the feather." In order to bear weight, that is, lightness must have a living source of power that allows it to exert force.

One of the engines of Lamarque's lightness may be found in her canny deployment of prosodic techniques often associated with children's literature, techniques that, as she deploys them, often have an uncanny effect: her sing-song phrasal repetitions seem not innocuous but destabilizing and unsettling, and her light-hearted rhythms and simple but unpredictable rhymes counterpoint and leaven with possibility her poems' complicated, heavy-hearted emotional themes. Vittorio Sereni, then one of the best known living Italian poets, glowingly reviewed *Teresino* when it first appeared, finding in her work "a continuous wellspring of analogies, a lightning-fast link between heart, mind, and memory, between the large and the imperceptible." He added that "sometimes two lines at the end of the most child-like ditty arrive without warning like a knife-blade." Such techniques, combined with her gift for storytelling and a grown-up wisdom rooted equally in innocence and experience, make her poems surprising, musical, and often, for me, indelibly memorable.

VIVIAN LAMARQUE : Four Poems

More and More You Seem

More and more you seem like a person in love
which I know has nothing to do with me
which I know has nothing to do with me.
That's why dinner went off the rails tonight
and why I'm spending so much
time now
washing these glasses.

The Matterhorn

Through iced-over windows
the Matterhorn was keeping his eye on me he knows
I call him as witness
he knows
that I had only you on my mind
how to put twice the flavoring in your broth to put meat on your bones
how to undress you undress me
how to teach you that line in German morgen will mein Schatz verreisen
how to escape with you in case of fire
how not to sink together into the snow
remember that ferocious dog?
he knows
that I told your sister in letters how happy I was
happy just like in photos.

Illegitimate Poem

Why are you crying, Stellina?
—Horace

That night I made love to you
in thought
I took no precautions
time passed and my thought grew
know that two nights ago
after painful contractions
I gave birth to an illegitimate poem
it will bear only my name
but has your foreign air and looks like you
you'd never guess it but it's true
you have a daughter.

Dear Name of Mine

Dear name of mine you leave me alone
with that companion who comes and goes
today she has stayed, casting her great shadow
over my mouth my mind
I'm scared she comes she goes she stays
she goes out bends down gets up buys petunias
she collects cats laughs has long hair
she wears glasses, do you think she's me
you tell her you're lonely.

I then dear name of mine
today I went and turned nine years old
or rather nine months in the mountains
or rather my mother is pregnant
or rather my mother is in love
dear name of mine I've remained there
I can't write you I'm not able.
How beautiful my mother in love
I gaze at her: I was never born.

—translated from the Italian by Geoffrey Brock

LAURA PAUL WATSON

Bolivian

They come weekly now, the infusions. More precisely,
I go to meet them. I sit in St. Anthony's lap
for three fluorescent hours,
the bags of medicine hung like jewels above my shoulder.
This one, from the yew tree, an opal, the way the sun hits it.
Four years ago it was pushed as a miracle.
But here, in my basement, the waning day-after,
the dexamethasone flushed from my system,
I'm a fixture on the couch. You yell downstairs
that there's a rainbow, and dear,
after sixteen years, I know exactly where, exactly how
it arcs over the ponderosa on the east side of the house
and drops one glowing end into the valley
where the willows tangle up its light
and the fishing pond and the fish repeat it.
I could hold up one trout
and see that rainbow a thousand times over.
If I would only find myself a window.
O, pots of gold. O, positivity.
I've seen those Hallmarks before, I've received them.
If you want a rainbow, you've got to put up with the rain.
Thanks, Dolly Parton. There's a procedural
auto-playing on the television, flashing a sick blue light
through the basement. My own rainstorm.
Mike Tyson would say I'm *fading into Bolivian.*
I could make a world out of that.

ECG

Who isn't driven inward here, the near dark. Who isn't glad
to spread their heart to the technician.
                              Lately, the news of myself
too much, I've looked elsewhere for some other suffering—

the day's news in the waiting room, Good Friday processions,
the Pope on the television saying *loving a thing is not enough*
to make it sacred.
                              I'm half-naked
and half-gowned. Even as I lie down, I'm still arriving,
still deciding how much and which of me has come today to her table.

I want to convince her what my heart is cut out for. I want to call myself beautiful,
these scars like ribbons running up and down my torso.

I shared the elevator up with a priest, dressed both Easterly and medicinal,
who, as I lie here, paces the hallways, checking names against his clipboard.

        The technician apologizes for the temperature.

Eleven, I first learned about metaphor—
how I was the Dead Sea and God's love was rotting inside of me.
Father Mooney said suffering was the point
of entry.
                How long I believed it—nothing good inside this body
reclined, now, in the dark, the altar of my memory glittering forth—
wounds gold dripping gold, eternally, and Father Mooney talking.

        How many times I asked to be opened up.

The technician patches me with electrodes, waves one hand
over the trackball and keyboard, the wand pressing against my ribs.

If my heart amounts to something, she'll say so, won't she.

I consider the switched-off fluorescents, bone-white, the gentle shells,
how, with the easiest touch, they shatter.

She sighs.
                                        Has difficulty.
My heart and its particular signal
is hidden in a mess of surgeries I forgot to warn her about.

Devout, healthy,
                        my grandmother gave all her money to the diocese.
(She loved me well enough, didn't she).
She listened to Father Mooney when he told her
my heart had no sense of the sacred. How long she believed it
I never asked.

                        I imagine her pacing the hallway
                        striking the error of my name from her clipboard.

The blinds of the exam room shimmy in the air conditioning, let in a little daylight.
It settles on the table, chest high. The wand looks up through my stomach.

Eventually she finds it, the technician, my heart.

TRACI BRIMHALL

A Group of Moths

is called a whisper, all those Xerxes flexing
blue apexes on the hush of a poppy's lip until
silence ushers them into a quieter fog. A group

of extinctions is called a grief or that one April,
our Kansas houses coated in dark wings, flutters
rushing down every chimney like sinking smoke.

Farmers say a group of miller moths is an infestation,
but dusted in fallen flour we spread the dead with
tweezers and call them a lesson, an aerial parade

of our missing. Some say a group of moths is called
an eclipse, and a group of eclipses is what I decide
to call a pandemic, suns shuttered like camera lenses,

and oh all the weeping behind walls before windows
open and the singing begins. But still others say a group
of moths is called a universe, each microscopic scale

the color of an exoplanet or dwarf star gathered into
a flight. A group of universes is called a family fever
or a dredge of lexicographers might say it is called

a worry, parents rocking to nocturnes of sonorous
moths, cupping a palm over a sleeping child's mouth
to feel the flame of breath gutter but keep burning.

DIANNELY ANTIGUA

Diary Entry #3: Study on the Negative

I want to be the prettiest bird on the internet
so I pretend they can see me through the motel mirror.
I practice lust, little loon on a bed of no love. The mirror says
my life is not worth the imitation of life. I am
not the favorite, I am not Noah. I am the dumpster
where I find the angel of the lord spelling my name with nothing
but fortune cookie crumbs, which is not to say
there is hope. No one will believe
it might be a disease making me beautiful
for a limited time. For a limited time, I don't have a will
or testament, but I have this never-ending
emptiness to give away like jewels. Don't
make me out to have value when all I can't do
is exist. I don't need to be a car flipped over on the side
of the road. I've romanticized displaying my mortality
like a da Vinci behind a red velvet rope—
the *Mona Lisa*, slightly awkward, the crowd taking pictures.

ALLISON ADAIR

Jubilee

More than the stiff architecture, the hard frame
with its inguinal striations or fistfuls of hair still
clasping tight to the scalp, more than the deep V
tensed as a flock of brazen geese migrating south
(bodybuilders call it "Adonis belt"), I miss a man's
need. The naked, essential helplessness he carries
beneath his breast pocket. The desperation—wild,
murderous—at a new lover's hand, shamelessly
pulsing so close to the crook of his violence. Don't
recall hearing a single clock tick, while swallowing
whole the symphony of crickets and cicadas outside,
their music of inhaled police whistles, distant bleating
goats, the click of a katydid's slack-wheel roulette.
Only the sound of a man exhaling so slow he grows
jealous, of himself—of his own milk-warm breath eddying
in fresh air spilling from some window suddenly propped
to winter. Wondering how the hell his luck managed to turn,
how he stumbled into this cave glittering with gold foil
and opals to be smoothed under a bold god's tongue when
all he'd done was zip his jacket and head out, hatless,
into the night, to see who else might be lonely enough
to watch the red and blue lights bless an accident beyond
the ridge, to pray in reckless rapture, buzzing cowlick
to tailbone, for a life of wanting: pure, unslakable thirst.

JAN BEATTY

Stripshot

I met a stripper on my first visit to the big West,
sitting on a hill in Marin—I was wearing a black red yellow plaid shirt,
she wore something more open, loose,
sleeveless.
        Her knees to her chest,
she was pulling at the brown California
grass, throwing it back down.
I loved looking at her plain brown hair falling over the side of her face.
I was still wearing women's clothes and shoes,
but I made myself a believer that day.
Her thick belt, heavy boots—brown eyes.

The way she looked at me until I had to look away.
She was *boy* and I hadn't met anyone like her yet,
look at her blue shirt, she opened me, the way
she tore at the grass: hard then threw it.
We walked the hills in Marin, I wanted
to be like her, I wanted to be her.
I couldn't even say what she had,
but I wanted it.
Our time lasted only weeks, but her face
still comes to me.

I made myself a queen those days,
inside I felt the turning diamonds
of a life not lived/someone's else's life,
now mine: holding the vision, heavy as mud,
I thought: *Just a push?*
Into my own bleeding heart—
I could feel the brass screws of the rail's underside/
a train running without me/
I could feel the spikes and the crosscuts
and I came alive in the fading light and the skyful of birds.

And I did, I did—and it was
fierce and wild, and back-to-the-wall scary,
it was off/on, whenever she was there, I was a blank slate
with a hard body, it was everything I wanted,
someone to kiss me nice and slow,
then slam me onto the ground's body.

It would be years until I knew her, knew that part of me
as I searched second-hand stores for men's clothing/
men's size 7 shoes, looking for the boy/man in me.
I don't believe in salvation, but
look at her body stripping:

jerking to one side, head bent,
hair covers her face, breasts large and moving,
her thickness:
Wet with boysweat between her legs,
a stripshot across a pitchblack stage,
flash of a woman running her show.
However she wants you/she can have you/half of a whole
body/stripping for you,
the body divided/
                              against itself
in beauty:
I made myself a man watching her:
the stripshot breaks apart
into millions of shotback stars
cutting the night apart
in her crosscut body,
hard and lovely.

Some people say half isn't anything/
but it will drive an ocean back
to the center.
She'll take your money and you'll thank her
in the cage of your body,
drowning in the stripping/
loving the shotback body.

Dear ghost of everything you wanted:

Jerking you into pleasure, jerking you
into your own story with a stripshot
of ammo to the vulva, triangle of light,
triangle of her: the wrapper, 3 sides of lust,
the fuckfield, the 4th eye.

I saw the future in her body but I didn't know my questions:
all that came out of my mouth
were birds.

REBECCA LINDENBERG

Chronic Illness Imagined as a Haunting

Origin of most of my chaos, ghost
hiding between the walls
of my cells   flickering the lights

the way a heart
stutters through a panic attack.

Since I'm eleven years old, constant
daily annoyances—

It's forever stalling or else
speeding up the clocks, fucking with

my sense of time, the way ten minutes
means something different

if you're furrowed over a new
recipe for béchamel
or waiting
for an ambulance.

Little things that, dementor-esque,
siphon off the life force:

Middle of the night, it shakes me awake
from the inside, or
because I'm hurrying

to a first day of teaching,
it'll hide all my test strips,
knowing that I cannot go without.

Like a poltergeist that'll steal the ace
from a full deck of cards
just to make it useless,

my ghost has a thousand ways
to ruin all the fun.

Blood sugar too high for a beer
on the brewery tour,
not a bite of the towering
carrot cake at my sister's wedding.

A miniscule crack in the insulin pump
lets just a tear's-worth of sea water in,
so it fails while we're snorkling

in Key West. It keeps beeping, beeping
on a boat full of sun-honeyed tourists
wondering what is that noise—

can't have any of the tropical
fruit plattered out in concentric crescents.

Can't get back to land (to fix this) any faster
than the captain is willing to go.

All the things you do to appease it—
not leaving a heel of bread on a sill
or passing the videotape along

but pricking my finger to draw a seed of blood,
plant it on a plastic strip—

Sometimes
I leave those around for my ghost to find.

Still, still   the ever-present sense of threat.

That it's loosening the blades
of the ceiling fan thumping in my chest,

doing its best to imbalance the bookshelves
of my hormones
I'll one day be found pinned under.

Or it'll push me down the staircase
of a low blood sugar and I'll
end up rag-dolled at the bottom.

Knowing it's hell-bent on my betrayal
I recite my lists of ways
that I might die,

which I'm always working on
so I can ghost-proof against them:

Could it fuck with the caulk, cause a leak,
moisten a joist so my bathtub-shaped
kidney falls?

That kind of insipid long-term shit
is just its style.

To anticipate it, I have detectors
everywhere—

Smoke, yes, and carbon monoxide, like everyone
but also devices
bespoke to my harassment.

A device to measure the rise and fall
of sugars in the body, another

to deliver the life-saving potion
that keeps the ghost in the blood quiet,
still another that just

makes the sound of a woman's voice

if I haven't spoken for awhile,
so I can haunt it back.

CYNTHIA BOERSMA

Little Cottage at the End of the Lane

The nights are endless now.
I've plenty of time to binge watch the British Baking Show
and start another jigsaw puzzle. The old don't sleep as much, you know.
The pictures can always be re-arranged.
My cat sleeps on my lap. From the couch
I see the neighbors' lights turn out, the glows
of screens subside. My house alone lights a dark street.
I keep the shelter here with the cat, eat some ice cream and drink a coke.
And take some comfort in another book on tape about the Holocaust.
Over the years, these books have piled in my memory attic
like hoarded towers of tabloids, crushing themselves,
crumbling and dissolving under their own weight.
My own story? The little mice nesting there. In the deep night,
when I am awake alone, I hear them scurrying about.
I turn up the volume. I let the cat out.

ANTHONY M. ABBORENO

Love Rituals

IT WAS A TRADITION FOR people in their city to row out on the lake and drown things they preferred to forget. Alan and Meredith both knew people who had done it. Old drinking buddies had rowed out the night after a binge to pour out the contents of their liquor cabinets; divorced couples had met for the last time to toss their wedding rings. Reminders of embarrassing secrets and words spoken in anger were committed.

Drowning love itself, however, had never been done. It was Alan who had found the key, stuffed in the back of a used paperback they had bought as a joke, on their second date: *Love Rituals: The Ties That Bind*. In it were instructions on how to strengthen love through bad poetry, or weaken it by taking the same poetry and jeering at its flaws. There were rituals for imposing love against another's will, and rituals for softening love's edges to better appreciate the notes within it, like a splash of water in good whiskey.

And then, in the very back, with warnings about the possible consequences, was a ritual for conjuring the very being of love. Because love is a living thing, multifaceted, different for every couple, and you can meet it if you wish.

Of course, the ritual warned that your love might not be the creature you'd expect. It could be sticky as candy left in a hot car. Or it could be a cruel thing, with barbed quills. Alan hadn't cared about either of those possibilities. He and Meredith were winding down from their most extreme argument yet, with shards of glass and pools of beer splashed across the kitchen floor, and pictures crooked on the walls. Their argument had raged throughout the apartment until they had finally settled in the living room, sitting on opposite ends of the couch, leaving sweat-stains on the cushions. Summer seemed to be getting hotter every year.

When Alan had been a child, his father had been a man without boundaries, so Alan had grown into someone who mistook aggravating bullshit for affection. This was the spirit in which Alan suggested performing the ritual. He expected Meredith to reject the idea—she hated woo, and other things she referred to as "fluffy stuff"—but to his surprise, she agreed.

She glared at him accusatorially. "I bet our love is a terrible conversationalist. I bet it tells long stories with no point, out of sheer malice, just to see people squirm."

Alan shook his head. "It doesn't matter how it talks, if we're just going to kill it."

Becalmed, they started their rites. They kept the windows closed so that the motes of energy could gather, and they burned incense left over from a failed experiment in moody romance. The ritual called for a goblet full of wine, which they didn't have, so they substituted a mug full of Old Crow, which they had to spit into and then sip from, as if they were not enacting an arcane rite but some adolescent hazing.

The smell, when the ritual was completed, was overwhelming, like being hotboxed in a van full of dirty underwear. Meredith opened the window and gasped for air, while Alan pulled his t-shirt over his nose.

Their love hovered in the center of the room, a blue mass like a glass sculpture. The air near it was cool, and when Alan reached towards it his hands came away damp, as if they had been sprayed with a fine mist. Patterns began to play across its surface, like wax in a lava lamp, the love's glow casting moving shadows against the walls. They watched, transfixed, as the patterns coalesced into something like a face—two eyes, a mouth opened wide as if preparing to speak.

Meredith didn't wait to hear what it might say. "Get a garbage bag."

Stuffing it away was easy. The bag felt slightly buoyant—as if there were a helium balloon inside it—so they added ballast: a pair of hand-weights for exercising, a Tupperware full of collected change, two cans of expired soup once intended for a food pantry. They tied the bag closed tightly, so that their love could not escape.

At the lake, they stared at each other. It was night, the water was murky green and flat, and the stone cliffs to the south loomed like an ancient congregation. They knew this would be the end, and after this moment there would be no resurrecting things. They might have been sick of love, but in truth their love had often been a beautiful thing, full of quiet joy and small kindnesses: full breakfasts on hungover mornings, love notes slipped in meals packed for work, song lyrics exchanged while running errands. They tossed the weighted bag into the lake and watched as bubbles rose while it sank, and when they looked at each other again, they were just people.

MURDERING LOVE IS not a small thing. Life moves on more quickly than if you had only allowed love to wither, in the normal fashion. When you are cleaning your home six months later and discover an earring, a dog-eared paperback, a t-shirt left behind, it does not provoke feelings in you. When a friend mentions how your former lover has married a real paranoiac, who collects knives, and thinks orange juice depletes his testosterone, it does not provoke more than the usual curiosity. You do not wonder if you left her worse off, open to people like this, or if this man in his brutalness is just another iteration of you, a fulfilment of the pattern she has repeated throughout her life. Years on, when you see her in the park with her children, you do not wonder what it would be like if they were yours.

Occasionally, you do glimpse your love in dreams. It appears to you as a different thing than you remember: a darkened outline, webbed with remorse, lingering at the edge of your vision after you awaken. By morning it is almost forgotten, junk mail you sort through while drinking your coffee.

FOR ALAN AND Meredith, as for many others, it was the drought that changed everything. The first signs of the drought were small—all the lawns in the town turned brown, except for the rich neighborhoods, where they stayed green. Coyotes were spotted wandering through peoples' yards, questing for water, and one woman awoke to discover a black bear in her kitchen, slurping from the faucet, his enormous arms wrapped around the sink like a drunk trying to quench the most painful hangover of his life.

The lake began to dry. People had to walk an extra five, then ten feet to reach the shore. They might notice the quality of the newly exposed ground, swollen from decades of water and now slowly contracting, like flesh rippled with stretch marks. And then one of the Baxter kids dove from a rocky outcropping into the southern pool, smashing his head to pieces.

It was tradition for children to dive there: the water had always been deep enough. But the Baxter kid's head had struck an old, metal locker someone had dumped decades before, judging by the discoveries inside it: a Buck Rogers space gun; a set of tin rocket-ships. Soon, other forgotten things appeared. Some of them were in containers—suitcases, jewelry safes, and even an old refrigerator. Others were in a state of near nakedness: weighted down with chains, stuffed into sections of metal pipe, or embedded in hunks of concrete.

Scavengers appeared, digging for treasure, but the value of nostalgia is relative. Biting flies gathered in clouds, and for most, the occasional wedding ring, with a glass diamond once passed as real, just wasn't worth it.

There were also rumors of something living in the deeper pools, the last parts to drain: something that had gone unnoticed while the lake was full but had found itself confined in the increasingly tiny space, like a prison cell. One persistent scavenger claimed that he had seen a glow coming from beneath the water, like a nightlight he remembered from childhood. Another claimed to have heard a sweet voice calling out, wordless and lonesome.

ALAN AND MEREDITH found each other in the discount supermarket, where they were not the only people wandering as though lost. People were crying by the frozen foods and staring listlessly at produce, and everyone's cart was filled with even more junk food than usual: twinkies, ice cream, and bags of foreign candies shaped like race cars, which they had found in the Daily Deals section.

Meredith did not have her kids with her, but it was obvious that she was shopping for a family, because her cart was brimming with discounted chicken thighs. Alan's cart held a six pack of non-alcoholic beer. He was trying to stay sober. Above them, a bad neon bulb flickered.

"I haven't had a good night's sleep since the Baxter boy smashed his head," Meredith said. "My kids need rides to school and little league games, the dishes need cleaning, and Henry, my husband, won't stop leaving his underwear on the floor. I need rest."

She reached into her purse and pulled out a pistol, just enough so that Alan could see it.

"I know it's little," she said, "the kind of thing women carry in their garters in old movies. But it can kill. Henry bought it for me while I was working downtown."

She replaced the pistol. "I've heard the scavengers who have stuck around can get a little rough. You might want to bring something for yourself."

That night, Alan dug through his house, looking for things that could serve as a weapon, but found that he didn't want to think about violence. The drying of the lake had shaken him, and he wanted to dwell on tenderness. Finally, he settled on a cast iron pan he and Meredith had used to cook together. He took a few practice swings with it in the living room, careful to ensure he didn't accidentally hit the TV, or break a lamp, and envisioned batting his love like a ping-pong ball.

THE NIGHT OF their rendezvous was dark, as promised. Moths seethed around Alan's headlights while he waited for Meredith to arrive. She pulled up shortly after, and jumped out of her truck.

She was wearing a headlamp and a shoulder holster, so she could keep her hands free. When she saw Alan's plastic flashlight and his frying pan, she shook her head. The flashlight was stamped with the name of a bail bonds office: a freebie for loyal customers.

"You better hope we don't get into real trouble," she said.

At the far side of the lake, they could see a couple of other peoples' flashlights bobbing, like tiny will-o-whisps. It would be easy to avoid them. They weren't looking for salvage, but headed towards the watery remainder.

On the way down, as Alan and Meredith skirted rusted junk and broken glass, they tried to pinpoint the moment that things had gone wrong between them. A year before the relationship ended, they had gone to the hospital to visit Meredith's father, who was dying of cancer. Alan had been drunk: he loved her father more than he had loved his own, and when he had broken down crying in the waiting room, Meredith's family had wasted time consoling him with coffee and candy bars from the vending machine, when they should have been saying their last goodbyes.

Now, Meredith explained. "Cancer is named after a crab, because that's what they used to think it was. Something armored, with its own motives, eating you from the inside while it makes itself larger."

The implication was clear: from Alan, Meredith had learned the necessity of growing her own armor and claws.

They heard something moving behind an old car, rusted out, its interior long rotted to a skeleton of wire and springs, and Meredith immediately adjusted to a firing stance, both arms holding her pistol in front, body turned to the side so as to present a smaller target for enemy fire.

"Hands up," she said.

A man staggered into the open. His beard was overgrown, and his clothes were muddy, as if he had been sleeping on the ground. "I don't have a weapon," he said. "I don't have anything."

Meredith did not lower her pistol. "It's not safe out here," she said, without irony.

The man winked. "It is very safe out here, as long as you are in love."

Alan heard a crunch behind him, the sound of somebody stepping on an aluminum can, and turned to see that two others had approached from behind. On top of their muddy clothes they had added adornments, dredged from the lake bottom—necklaces, rings and bracelets, racked up in rows. One was a man and the other a woman, and the woman was wearing two hats—a mildewed baseball cap, and on top of that, a Stetson with a crushed brim.

Meredith glanced over her shoulder and her hands trembled. Alan knew the look. She wanted to kill everyone—him too—and wash her conscience of everything.

But then, a familiar smell enshrouded them all. It seemed to seep from the mud. Alan caught it first, and recognized it immediately as the smell from their apartment that long ago afternoon, when they had decided their love needed to die. Back then, it had revolted him, but with the passage of time it had become nostalgic.

It had a calming effect on Meredith as well. She relaxed her shoulders, lowered her pistol, and looked at Alan. Aches and pains they had acquired over the years seemed to lift. Alan's bad knee, from when he had stumbled and fallen drunk in the first week after the murder? Gone. The pain in Meredith's lower back, which had come during her first pregnancy and never vanished? Gone. Suffering felt diminished by a new sense of possibility.

The first of the scavengers nodded when he saw the look on their faces. "We came here hoping for treasure, but instead we found something better. Come with us."

They followed the scavengers over a hill covered in beer bottles and dead fish, the stink of rotting meat blending seamlessly with the stink of love. At the top of the hill, more scavengers had gathered, each more extravagantly adorned than the last, some with accoutrements generations out of fashion—monocles and pocket watches and dirty cummerbunds. Rules of taste or convenience were ignored. Each object was its own perfect masterwork, as worthy and necessary as any other.

Below the crest of the hill, at the center of a basin, lay a stagnant pool. Moths fluttered, drawn by the glow, as pale arms long as tree trunks reached from the water and love drew itself up and out into the night, a head and spider limbs, a face with deeply carved eye sockets and vestigial nose and benign smile. When it had reached its full height, it towered over everyone like the moon come to Earth. It had been naïve to think that love could be murdered. Like many things, it could only be hidden, and once hidden had continued to grow.

Meredith raised her gun and shivered, but before she could fire Alan grabbed her hand. He leaned in close, as though preparing to dance the tango, and their love encroached, its clammy aura permeating the air. If you asked Alan what the love was seeking, he would say "forgiveness." And if you asked Meredith, she would say "revenge."

Instead, love's aura took them further back, to when the lake was unlike this. Alan and Meredith had visited in better times, when the water was deep, and jet skis lashed the waves.

There was Alan, in a pair of ten-dollar Wal-Mart trunks decorated with tiki masks and tropical drinks, and there was Meredith, in her floral two-piece, lying on beach blankets faded from washing. Both were unarmored, smelling like coconut sun lotion that was too weak, and their skin was beginning to redden and burn. The sun was unseasonably hot. Even the sky seemed desiccated and yellow, slashed with clouds from a passing plane.

Later, Alan and Meredith would lie in bed, with skin that was already beginning to blister and peel, and each would blame the other for the pain. If Meredith hadn't insisted that she did not like the smell of the stronger lotion. If Alan hadn't wanted to be so cheap. But in their moment together at the beach, everything was perfect. Alan put his hand on Meredith's and clasped it tightly, looking towards the cliffs on the lake's opposite shore. If he squinted, he could see a group of boys playing—taking turns running across the rocks, and diving into the waves.

Translation Folio

SAADI YOUSSEF

Translator's Introduction

Khaled Mattawa

FROM TIME TO TIME, OVER the past two decades of his life, Saadi Youssef and I chatted on Skype—exchanging news, talking about poetry, and commiserating about the sad fate of our countries. In these conversations, I often found myself listening to an unwritten chapter of modern Arabic poetry, as if a time portal had opened onto a strange and interesting past I knew nothing of. Talking with Saadi was like playing with Russian dolls, finding a story inside another story and another inside that—where the fine details are the main story, and what you hear as a free-standing story is really the first chapter of a novel. Saadi, a deep imagist who wrote every day and who spoke and recited his terse poems in what seemed like a whisper, was nonetheless a spiritual descendant of Shahrazad, the narrator of *The Thousand and One Nights*.

I started translating Saadi in the early 1990s and communicated with him by snail mail via an address in the Ministry of Tourism in Amman, where he had been granted a job—a consultancy I presumed, because he was never there when I called to make sure he got my letters. A refugee for more than a decade by then, he still traveled a great deal. But I did eventually get replies to all my queries, and I slogged on with my translations. In 2000, he moved to London and was given political asylum and council housing. He'd fully furnished his tiny apartment and decked it out with a great many knickknacks and framed pictures—all the signs of a person intent on making a home—all or most acquired from flea markets at a cost of no more than 200 pounds, according to him. All the signs of a person who's lived in near poverty most of his life.

The volume of selected poems by Saadi that I completed in the early 2000s, *Without an Alphabet, Without a Face* (Poems 1952–1997), was published by Graywolf in 2003, at the onset of the second war on Iraq, which was bitterly ironic. The book helped raise Saadi's profile, and after a few readings together, I began to see him traveling the world to read his poems in Arabic and sometimes my translations. At times he was accompanied by another translator reciting translations of my translations into another language. It was gratifying to see such a great poet take flight with the aid of my renderings of his lines.

I don't know exactly when our Skype conversations began, but they became regular during the Arab Spring in 2011, when he became worried about my lengthy stays in Libya. Saadi was also dubious about the rebellions and predicted that the countries of the region would fall to the same fate as his Iraq—destruction by Western powers, followed by civil war, refugees, and failed states. He listened to my optimistic take on things and relayed his worries and his deep concern for me. In London, he was writing up a storm; he wrote more there, he once told me, than he'd written in all his five previous decades as a poet. It was hard to keep up with his books—perhaps there were too many, I thought to myself, or they were too focused on what was happening in the muddled politics of post-Saddam Iraq. I didn't have enough time to read or translate him, and he was fine with that. He never stopped checking on me, which I loved him for.

Then in 2014 *Banipal* magazine was preparing an issue on Saadi and wanted to know if I'd like to translate a few of his recent works. The poems were gorgeous. They had the hallmarks of his poetry: precise images and diction, short poems that generated tension through the impartial focus that Saadi brought to whatever he saw before him or felt inside him. The poems were acts of discovery and revelation marked by a probing sensibility, like that of a hunter, perhaps, who relies on witnessing as a means of sustenance. The outcomes varied. Some poems ended on tragic notes; others were self-deprecating. He knew he was aging and spending his last years in exile. Both of these specters haunted him—and perhaps interrogated him, so that his poems seemed like he was attempting to answer the nagging questions posed to him.

The last time I saw Saadi in-person was on New Year's Day of 2020. I had begun to translate him again, having finished a book of my own poems that took me ten years to write. I was again fit to take on Saadi's work, and I was hoping to collaborate with him on the translations, this time going over them together via Skype. And we did that in the following year. During that last time we were together, in which he gifted my daughter a set of Russian dolls, Saadi showed me a manuscript of fifty sonnets that he'd just completed. He talked about the difficulties he'd faced in translating Walcott, which he'd ultimately had to give up. And as we prepared to leave, Saadi handed me a copy of his translations of Li Po (based on English versions). Saadi asked me if I knew the poem "The River Merchant's Wife," by Ezra Pound, which is a loose translation of a poem by Li Po. Indeed, I said, and I know the story well of how Pound made his mark as a poet with those poems in *Cathay*.

In the doorway of his tiny apartment, Saadi said that Badr Shakir al-Sayyab's translation of Pound's translations of Li Po's poems—especially "The River Merchant's Wife"—had been a revelation to him when he'd first encountered it. He explained that they'd borne the unmistakable techniques and aspirations of the sort of modern poems he'd wanted to write, but until then had not known how. His new translation of Li Po, even though it came to Arabic via English, was an homage to the great Chinese bard and to al-Sayyab, who helped him find his voice. Saadi was reaching back, reaching to his beginnings, not with a sense of nostalgia, but in order to begin again.

During that last visit, while I chatted with Ikbal, Saadi wife, who was a leading actress and director in Iraq, she told me that Saadi has had some health issues and had been hospitalized on a few occasions as of late. It was not clear what was ailing him, but in June 2021 he died of cancer.

In my mind, that visit with Saadi and Ikbal continues like an endless reel of stories, laughter, food, and more stories. I remember at one point glancing at Saadi as he talked to my daughter with great curiosity and joy, and the reasons I loved him flashed before me like a flock of snow geese taking off from a winter lake, countless and ever-returning.

SAADI YOUSSEF : Four Poems

At The Café Drinking Black Coffee

Who knew
that the depth of the sea would be my anchor
and now it's dragged me away.
I wake up dazed,
can't fix my eyes on anything,
my steps don't know where to go.
And the sky is dense,
rain,
cold lead,
dry lips.
Sometimes, I think that my favorite song is:
To die . . .
As the seaweed dies,
green . . .
Do you think life is a good thing?
I mean:
Is it worth living through?
I'm tired . . .
Tell the truth, Maisoon.
Give me some advice:
Should I go on swinging and twisting
between prophecy and madness?

Harbor

Dusk,
and the town square is desolate,
but the rain
and the lamps
have spread a wide shining lake
on the abandoned square.
A harbor is being born.
....
....
....
Is it time to set sail again?

Cliff Edge Café, Tangier

(Founded in 1921)

Like a terrace on a hill
the cafe leans toward the sea
as if about to plunge into the water
to take the café's boys and girls to the opposite shore.
Spain looms in the cloud-muddled horizon,
but the café will still numb
whoever enters it
with scents from paradise:
mint,
hashish from the Rif,
local tobacco,
and dark perfumes from the girls' armpits.

Lullaby

Whenever I'm fed up with the earth, I seek water.
There, by the canal, which has neither
an outlet nor source,
I surrender my body.
My rapid breathing calms,
my eyes release their fatigue.
And when light waves glide along the little lotus flower
I hold my wrist
and count my pulse.
Calm down.
Calm down.
I close my eyes,
happy that I've distanced myself from earth,
that I'm wading in water
toward the end of that canal,
which has neither outlet nor source.

—translated from the Arabic by Khaled Mattawa

RANDY F. NELSON

Citizen of a Momentary World

When Mr. Navabi arrived at the new address, suitcase and documents in hand, he knocked at the door wondering what variety of Americans would be on the other side. He hoped they would be kind and understanding, but he was prepared for hardship as well. The house itself was small, two single-paned windows on either side of a blue door. There were three steps up to a concrete porch with a broken railing, plus a plastic tricycle with one pedal missing. But Mr. Navabi was not discouraged. He knocked a second time, thinking *I will fix the railing first and then paint the house after a paycheck or two. And, later on, perhaps something for the children.* Their names, he recalled, were Tomás and Sofia. The wife would be, yes, Fabiana. And if there were others inside, he would win them over as well.

A mocha-skinned woman answered the door. She pronounced the word *yes?* with an accent that Mr. Navabi could not recognize. Still, for a moment, he simply beheld her, luxuriating in his good fortune. She was delicate and beautiful, with dark eyes to match his own and a face so open and kind that he wondered what misfortune had raised an angry red welt below her left eye. She held the door open only a few inches as if expecting bad news, and she carried a blanket-wrapped toddler on her hip. The baby removed a pacifier from its mouth and reached for Mr. Navabi as if he had rocked her to sleep the night before. It was a good sign he thought. So he took the top two pages from his packet of documents and passed them to the woman saying, "Good afternoon, madam. I am the new Richard."

She did not take the papers and edged herself further behind the door. "Are you the police?" she said.

"No, madam. I am not the police," Mr. Navabi replied. He kept his voice calm and polite, understanding that this transition would be challenging for the family and that Fabiana—if this was Fabiana—would be worried if she had not been properly notified.

"What do you want?" she said. This time with real alarm.

"Why, to come inside. To unpack my things. And to . . . begin."

"If you don't have a warrant," she said, "please go away. You're at the wrong address, and we don't know you. We don't know anyone who sounds like you. This is the wrong house." Fabiana began to close the door. It looked to Mr. Navabi as if she were about to break into tears, as if he himself were the last in the very long line of afflictions that constituted her life.

Before either of them could speak again, a long black car turned into the street and crept past the first few houses. It was a BMW sedan that looked so out of place in the neighborhood that Mr. Navabi winced when its right front tire dropped into the driveway puddle and splashed filth over the hard obsidian shine. *Perhaps some gravel and cement* he thought. *I will have to fix that hole before winter when freezing and thawing will make it worse.* The car stopped inches from the porch and a tall woman got out.

"Sorry," the woman said. "Sorry. There was a mix-up. I'll bet we're all a little confused right about now." She smiled with a burst of whiteness as intense as a photographer's flash. She wore black glasses and a dark business suit that exaggerated her height. Her fingers went marching over a small computer tablet while she made her way to the porch.

"If you are the police, tell this man to leave," said Fabiana.

The woman from the car examined Mr. Navabi as if checking his driver's license. Then she studied her tablet with the same intensity and finally examined Mr. Navabi again. After a full minute, she drew a deep, satisfied sigh. "Why don't we step inside?" she said. Without waiting for an answer she eased herself through the narrow opening and drew Mr. Navabi in her wake. "Olivia Leonitis," she announced in the tiny hallway. "I'm with the Bureau."

"What is happening?" Fabiana said. "What does this mean?"

"Okay, the old Richard. The old one, is being replaced, sweetie. I can promise you that. Believe me, he'll be someone else's problem. The Bureau absolutely guarantees that. —Now, the *new* Richard? He just arrived a little early. So, again, sorry about that. Case overload. Anyway, we'll go over the details in a minute; but, trust me, your life is going to be much, much better than it was."

Mr. Navabi looked at his new surroundings. He heard Fabiana voicing some kind of objection and Mrs. Leonitis replying with a long explanation and further assurances. After another exchange or two, the words of both women seemed to fade into the background as Mr. Navabi took in the full extent of his good fortune. A miracle really. The house itself was just as they had told him, one promise already fulfilled. He was amazed. Four rooms. Wooden floors. Plumbing. A kitchen table with two chairs. A cloth rug of many colors in the room where they were standing. What kind of man was the old Richard that he would spoil such a life? This was America, where they made electricity for both day and night. I will be the new Richard, Mr. Navabi assured himself. A new man. And I will make this family happy and proud once again. Still, he felt the first twinge of uneasiness himself. The Bureau had promised that his own family would follow him to America, but the current misunderstanding? It seemed that more than a detail or two had been muddled.

"Let me ask you this," Mrs. Leonitis was saying to Fabiana. "Would it help your, let's call them, concerns. Would it help your concerns if I replaced that"—she pointed to a dented appliance in the kitchen—"with a new washing machine? Think of it as your first step toward that better life. You want a better life for your kids, don't you?"

Mr. Navabi wanted a better life for the children as well. He set down his suitcase as Fabiana kept insisting that she would not have a stranger in her house, and he took a step further into the gloom as Mrs. Leonitis pointed out that this was not Fabiana's house. A chair revealed itself. Mr. Navabi had never seen such a chair. It was a very large, puffed pastry of a chair with no rockers that nevertheless rocked, forward and back, as if propelled by something inside its cavity. And even more surprising was the very old man, with a decaying smile, seated in the chair. Thin and grey from lack of sunlight, his arms motionless on the bloated arms of the chair. Forward and back he went as the two women recited their misgivings. Mrs. Leonitis was saying think of this as a boarding house. Think of yourself as the boarding house matron, at least here at first. And at the same time Mr. Navabi was wondering if the old man was the father of Fabiana or some apparition. He raised one hand in a kind of salute to the seated figure, but the other did not acknowledge him or change expression.

The conversation between the women was reaching a climax Mr. Navabi realized, because Fabiana had raised her voice; and a little boy, perhaps seven, had emerged from one of the back rooms. The boy stood in the compressed hallway, alert but at a safe distance from the argument. Tomás, thought Mr. Navabi. A handsome boy who stood rigidly, breathing through his mouth in irregular sips. Surely this was not the introduction that a child should have to his new father. A family quarrel before they had become a family?

It all ended with a sudden, sharp exchange. Whatever Fabiana had been saying went beyond the patience of Mrs. Leonitis. The latter stopped herself in mid-sentence and held up one hand as if halting traffic. In cold, clear syllables she said. "Do not forget, my dear, that you are yourself. Very. Easily. Replaceable."

It subtracted Fabiana down to tears. She dropped her head, nodded once, and ran past the boy. Mrs. Leonitis muttered good luck to Mr. Navabi and left. The old man in the chair rose up slowly, following Fabiana. And the new Richard took his place. The boy turned stiffly, perhaps fearfully, toward the still open door of his room.

•

In the kitchen there was a refrigerating machine, an electric stove, a sink with a dripping faucet, and an overhead light that cast a yellow glow over the countertops. The one window above the sink had gone opaque with the gathering darkness outside. Mr. Navabi found a coffeepot, filled it with water, and set it on the stove. Then he went looking through cabinets as he waited for the water to boil. He didn't hear the old man come back into the kitchen.

"Beer in the fridge," the old man said. "Maybe some sandwich stuff too. She won't be coming out tonight, I can tell you that much." His words were followed by the sound of a chair being pulled back from the table and someone sitting down. "So what's your real name anyhow? Where you from originally?"

Mr. Navabi turned and examined the man whose reappearance was as puzzling as the argument in the living room. In the wan light, the man seemed tubercular and frail rather than old. His face looked as if it had been drawn on crumpled paper, and his voice sounded mildly threatening. He wore faded jeans and a white t-shirt that drooped at the neck.

Mr. Navabi answered him by reciting the correct information, "My name is Richard Kolchak, from Pittsburgh. In Pennsylvania. My parents emigrated to this country from Central Europe in nineteen. . . ."

"God no, not that shit. I mean, what's your real name?"

Mr. Navabi knew he should not hesitate, but he could not help feeling uncertain about his awkward introduction. A bit too late he said again, "Richard Kolchak."

"Look, you want this to work out, right? Become a permanent thing? Let me tell you, you ain't going do it by reading back some script they gave you."

"Please, I have come from a very long way," said Navabi.

"Look, I'm not trying to screw up your deal. I'm just curious, that's all."

"I was told not to deviate."

"Yeah? Well, how's that working out for you?"

"I have textile experience," Mr. Navabi said with some force. "I have been a weaver, a loom fixer, and a warehouse man. I can drive a lift truck. And also drive a regular truck. And operate a stacking machine. And, before that, I worked in the carding room and in doffing. I am *very* qualified to be here. And I can learn."

"That's where they're going to put you? In the textile mill? Pay you the same thing you was making in Outer Pakistan?"

"Lebanon," corrected Mr. Navabi. "I am from Lebanon. Although, actually, my family are from Syria; but the war happened, as you may know. Then they found me at a camp in Minyeh. The Bureau did. For which I am very grateful, and I do not question when God smiles on me. And so, may I ask, who are *you*?"

"Nobody very qualified, I can tell you that."

The water began to boil, and Mr. Navabi took down a cup from one of the cabinets, then retrieved a box of tea from his suitcase. "This was to be a present for Fabiana," he said, "but I do not think she will mind." He stirred the steaming cup with a spoon he found lying next to the sink. The other man watched him from a remoteness that Mr. Navabi could not fathom. For a time neither of them spoke. Then the baby in the far room cried once, and they could hear soothing sounds coming from behind the thin wall. A muffled melody reached the kitchen and eased whatever tension had been building between the men. Mr. Navabi took from his suitcase a stuffed rabbit made of terrycloth and also a miniature soccer ball. "For the children," he said.

A look of impenetrable sadness came upon the older man; and he rose up from the table, crossing to the refrigerator where he opened the door and peered into the cold cascading air with his back to Mr. Navabi. He came back to the table with a beer and made wet circles on the laminate between sips, wiping them away with his free hand. Finally he said in an altered voice, "Yeah, that boy loves to play ball. He'll like that."

Mr. Navabi did not know what to say. He had the feeling that they had blundered past some unknowable hostility between them. There was less anger and suspicion in the room, and he felt he should not let the moment go by without some sign of good will. Then he thought of offering the man something from his former life. "Ashar," he said at last. "My real name is Ashar Navabi."

The man tilted his beer bottle toward Mr. Navabi and tapped the lip of the tea cup before taking a long drink. Then he said, "Pleasure. —Richard. —Kolchak. But I reckon you already knew that."

"I am you?!"

"I think technically you aren't supposed to be me quite yet. But I'll be outta your hair soon enough. So don't look so worried. People disappear all the time. Besides, you got the i.d. now. Social security, birth certificate, photographs, work records, DNA match. Everything. They're that thorough. I couldn't prove I was me to my own mama. How much did all that cost you?"

"I have to work off the debt. In the mill, for a time."

"Well, Richard. Welcome to the new me. Would it surprise you to learn I was the one who asked for the replacement? Not her."

Mr. Navabi did not know what to say. Such a statement coming so casually from the rumpled man was inconceivable. He could not imagine that anyone in America would be unhappy. Mr. Navabi looked down at the table, embarrassed for his host's naiveté. Soon the singing and cooing sounds from the bedroom stopped, and the dark chasm grew. Finally the first Richard Kolchak said, "I just want you to know it was never about the work. I could always handle the work. Better than most I expect."

"Then why?"

Another hesitation, this time a much longer one. Then, "The boy. Tomás. Fabiana's boy. —I'm pretty sure they're gonna to replace him too."

Mr. Navabi could not believe what he was hearing. A sliver of fear wheedled itself into his consciousness. "But why?" he said. "Who would replace a child?"

"They would. Anyway, he's not really mine. Although I guess in a way he is."

"But *why* though?"

"He's real sick. Expensive sick. But the why of it don't matter. What I'm trying to tell you is just because I'm a drunk and a coward don't mean I got no feelings. I just wanted you to know that."

•

Mr. Navabi, the new Richard, felt immediately at home in the textile mill. The vinegary smell hovering over the dye house was at once familiar to him, and its trickle of discharge water he recognized as well. It was the cobalt blue of hard-pressed denim. He set to work in the picking room where he binned cloth in storage racks before orders were gathered and shipped. It was a solitary job that took him through long, dusty catacombs where he stacked rolls of cloth until they resembled corpses he had seen in mass graves outside Aleppo.

Later, in Mr. Navabi's second week, inspectors from the Bureau replaced several of the old binning carts and a binner named Kutchenko. Production improved. It was less than another month when a new, unfamiliar inspector found him in one of the farthest aisles and said "Kolchak?" Navabi was putting up an undyed roll of slub which he cradled in his arms and, without thinking, answered, "Yes." The inspector kept playing a small flashlight over the bins as if expecting the rolls to unravel and crawl forth. Finally he found his voice and spoke fondly of the new Richard's energy and attitude. He wanted to know if he was ready to move up. Did he think he could drive a forklift? It would mean an extra dollar an hour.

Again he said yes, bowing slightly with gratitude. Yes, he was ready indeed.

"Good" was the reply. "See your supervisor at the end of shift. Tell him you are replacing Ordoñez."

"Good," said Navabi. *Surely the increase in pay will purchase a kind of peace with Fabiana.*

But it was not that easy.

At home Fabiana spent most of her time with the baby. She and the children slept in one bedroom, Navabi in the other. He dreamed occasionally of his own wife and children awaiting their chance for America, but he could not believe he was being cruel by taking another's place. Worse things happened every day in the camps. New people arrived, old ones disappeared, and your identity became whatever piece of paper moved you farther along. It was a process, like an assembly line. You simply lived inside the world given to you. He found it strange that Americans could not see this.

It was the boy, Tomás, who finally changed all their lives. He adored Navabi.

The two of them played with the soccer ball in the scabby, sloping yard where Navabi demonstrated simple tricks from his own childhood, flipping the ball over his shoulder with a rainbow toss or holding a footstall for minutes at a time. But even the basics eluded the boy. When he ran, he could barely bend his knees. When Navabi tried to teach, the boy seemed not to hear. And yet they played, Tomás making incomprehensible sounds of delight, while Navabi tried not to recall the natural agility of his own son, Sabir. Fabiana grew less distant even as she continually cautioned them away from the street. "He's nearly deaf," she said. "He can't hear the cars or words unless you shout." On ordinary days the boy attended a special school, and at night he made signs with his hands that only his mother understood.

It became their habit for Navabi to lift both boy and ball to his shoulders when headed back to the house for dinner, Tomás so rigid with terror and delight that he sat like a statue. Finally one evening he asked Fabiana the plain and pointed question. What is wrong with your son? How is he expensively sick?

"It's rare," she said. "A long word. Incurable. It means his joints are turning into solid bone. Other tissues too. Someday he will not be able to move or breathe." She said this without crying and without expectation that Navabi would care. It surprised her that he seemed so affected. Thereafter, she packed his lunch in the mornings, touched his shoulder when he said goodnight.

On another evening Fabiana asked him about his own family and watched Navabi slip from his usual politeness into a kind of despair that she mistook for loneliness. "What are their names?" she said. "Do you have children, and do you miss them at all?"

"You think I'm not quite human," he said. "And of course I miss them. A boy. A girl."

"And a wife I suppose?"

"Yes, Kameela." He hesitated, then added, "It means 'perfection.'" Navabi reached into his back pocket and took out a leather wallet. "They don't allow photographs to be brought over," he said. "The Replacement Bureau I mean. But I have this one that I saved." He unfolded a piece of paper, badly creased and printed in fading colors. It resembled a postcard from another century and showed a street scene in front of the tents and the chaos of a crowded encampment. At the left extremity was an outdoor butcher's shop with a man hacking at something on a wooden table. Women in dark clothing dominated the background while in the center of the picture baskets of bread, a metal water tank, and a small cooking fire attracted the attention of so many others that a young woman walking through the foreground, blurred by her pace, hardly appeared at all. To Fabiana she was nearly invisible, a ghost out of Navabi's past.

"What are your children's names?" she asked.

"My son, Sabir. He is a good boy. He wants to go to university someday. They said it was possible. In America. And my daughter Nalani."

"Sabir."

"Yes."

"And when they bring him over?"

"They told me he would be Tomás," he said. "But back then it was only a name."

•

MRS. LEONITIS CHECKED her office alerts and found a disturbing message that required her attention. It seemed that a young woman from one of the affluent neighborhoods had been spreading rumors, insisting really, that her father was not her father. It took several telephone calls for Mrs. Leonitis to locate the girl, Elizabeth Fenton, at Prospect Academy, then another few calls to have her taken out of class and put in a private room where she and Mrs. Leonitis could talk. The new father had apparently not been an ideal placement, and the girl was being a teenager. Petulant, sulky, disagreeable.

Mrs. Leonitis met the principal first and was directed to a guidance counselor's office that had been vacated for the interview. It was late in the day and a sliver of sunlight through the half-closed blinds fell on a heavy-set girl with auburn hair and a glowering expression. She sat on a brown sofa several feet from the counselor's desk. The room itself was barely large enough for two people and packed with college posters and uneven stacks of paper. Mrs. Leonitis closed the door, then propped herself against the front of the desk and smiled. "Elizabeth," she said. "You look unhappy. Do you know who I am?"

"You're one of them," the girl said.

"Good. Yes. Now—. You seem disturbed, and I've heard that you've been sharing some unpleasant feelings with your friends."

"You don't have to talk to me like I'm a baby."

Mrs. Leonitis nodded and kept her tone conversational. "I'm just wondering if the arrangements weren't made clear to you."

"He's not my father," Elizabeth Fenton announced.

"But the arrangements. They were explained to you at the time, and you clearly understood them, am I right?"

Then a sudden burst of vehemence from the girl. "He's not my father! He's not Ray Fenton!"

Mrs. Leonitis tilted her head and gave a show of concern. "Has he been unkind to you, or has he done something inappropriate?"

The girl made a disgusting face. "Ew. No. Why is that all adults ever think about?"

"We want you to be safe and happy," said the tall woman, now standing upright. "And for our town to be safe and happy. Have you talked to your mother about this?"

"I want to know where he is. My real father. I want to know where you sent him."

Want, Mrs. Leonitis thought. *All of them. They want.* "You've been very public with your concerns," she went on. "That makes things difficult for us all. No one is forced to come in. No one is forced to leave. The Replacement Bureau is a private consulting group that has been helping to bring immigration and inefficiency under control."

"Where is he?" the girl demanded.

"Someplace nice. I promise."

"But why? Nobody asked me what *I* wanted."

"Elizabeth, adults step aside for many reasons. You know that. Divorce. Illness. Job insecurity or simple boredom. Some people just walk away. It's a difficult, competitive world we live in. And adults sometimes have to make difficult decisions. The Bureau smooths those over as well as we can. All this was explained to you in the counseling sessions."

"They weren't *divorced*! I just want to know where he is!"

"I've already told you. Someplace very nice."

Elizabeth Fenton sank back into herself, her plaid skirt dipping between her knees and one foot pressing against the other ankle. She looked into the fading sunlight of the narrow window and tried to imagine the rest of her life. "I don't want to be here," she said. "I don't want to be in this town."

"I understand," said Mrs. Leonitis. "But you'll feel differently as you get older."

"I don't want to *be* in this town. I want to be with my dad. My real dad."

"Your real dad is Ray Fenton. He is at home waiting for you. Right now. Why don't we call your mom and . . . ."

"No! She's happy with the whole thing. Just like the rest of you. But I want *out*!"

Mrs. Leonitis drew a deep sigh. "I understand."

"No you don't! Nobody does! Nobody will even talk about it."

"You're saying you'd like a change. And I can make that happen, Elizabeth. But is it what you'd really like? Would you like to be replaced?"

"I hate it here!" the girl insisted.

"If that's the way you feel. I can begin making arrangements, but you need to understand that they'll be permanent. Are you sure?"

"I want to be with my dad."

"Of course. We can do that for you. We can send you to someplace nice."

Afterwards Olivia Leonitis felt she had done her best for the girl and for the Bureau. The welfare of the town was what mattered. The descent into poverty, the filth, the hopelessness of deserted streets was what the bureau wished to avoid. Even people in the lower strata saw the numbness and the dull finality of nearby towns. There was a certain pride in Delmont, Mrs. Leonitis reflected, an energy not found anywhere else within the region. It puzzled her, though, that as she left the school it was the principal who seemed afraid. Not the girl.

•

EACH EVENING AT the hour of prayer Mr. Navabi recited his sins. *I have stolen another name's name. I have invaded his house. I have looked upon his wife. I have lifted up his son in my arms. And each day I tell another lie.* After a time the words became a mantra which he muttered quickly because these sins did not strike Navabi as absurd. He had seen much worse in the camps where depravity was the norm.

Nevertheless, he set out to make his present circumstance bearable in the only ways he knew how. He sowed grass in the bald spots of the yard. He planted a tree. He fixed the railing of the front porch as he had promised and dug out the pothole in the driveway filling it with a mixture of gravel and cement. He asked Fabiana if she would like the kitchen painted; and she looked at him as though he had posed a riddle. When she blinked and said nothing, he offered *blue?* Then finally, after a long moment, she said *white* as if the word had come at the end of a much longer conversation. Thereafter and throughout the autumn they treated each other like neighbors, nodding every morning before work, saying *excuse me* in their separate languages when they passed in the hall.

One evening in early December Fabiana reverted to English when she said *sit* as Navabi came into the kitchen. She intended it as a joke because the day before he had offered to buy a puppy for the children. What surprised everyone though, perhaps Fabiana most of all, is that she had already filled a plate for him and set it, not unkindly, in front of him at the table. Then she watched him eat, just as the women did in her former country.

Several evenings later, during a second meal that they shared, her hand accidentally brushed his when she set the plate before him. And for the first time he felt himself at ease inside the newly painted kitchen. After that dinner, Fabiana took a chair at the table instead of clearing away the dishes. With Sofia on her lap, she stroked the child's hair while she and Navabi talked, their first full conversation since he had arrived. They talked about everything but their former lives.

In the week before Christmas, Navabi worked double shifts at the mill. Each night Fabiana left the light on for him in the tiny hallway because he got home after eleven. It was there that she met him on the evening that the snow began to fall. He arrived cold and tired, bending over to remove his shoes just after closing the front door, and so he did not notice her until he looked up again. She was standing just outside the bathroom, a visible cloud of steam behind her and a towel covering her torso.

Navabi looked away. When he moved toward his room, he put his back against the wall and attempted to sidestep around her in their usual way but somehow they were touching before he reached the door. Sandalwood and citrus rising from her hair. The doorframe itself pressed them further together, her body fully against his; but he did not realize he was being led until the towel fell away and he saw that his cot had been made up with clean linens and turned down as in a hotel.

A small lamp on the dresser gave the only light after the door was closed. Fabiana unbuttoned his shirt and then left the rest to him as she placed herself beneath the covers. "I do not mean to be a difficult woman," she said. "I mean to make this life work."

An apology? he wondered. Because she did not strike him as the type of woman who would easily let herself fall in love.

At first he simply laid beside her, grateful for the warmth and softness, a momentary stay against the cold. He closed his eyes, breathed out, and nestled his head into the pillow. "We need each other," she said. "It is cold. And we are poor. And . . . we need each other." Then he said something in return, and in another moment he was kissing her lips and breasts, keeping one hand at her hips to bring her even nearer. The deeper warmth of her was shocking to him, and her own urgency made him whisper things he'd never thought to say before. Perhaps it was the cold itself that kept them together long after they had exhausted each other. Neither of them could say. But when she finally left Navabi's room, it was near dawn; and she picked up the towel from the floor drying the hair between her legs and then wrapping it around her tightly. She did this facing him, and he watched her realizing that they had crossed a line that he'd never imagined in his haste to take a spot in America. "We may as well stop pretending" is all she said. And he nodded, not able to name the emotion flooding through him or to acknowledge the confusion. He decided that it was not love that had taken hold of him; but Navabi wondered if this was how the world's first love had begun, eons ago, in the time of ice and fire at the mouth of a cave.

"We'll make it work" is what he said.

"We'll make it work," she replied, closing the door as she left.

For a long time Navabi lay next to the damp impression in the bed. He breathed in the faint scent of her, trying to establish the memory in his mind. When at last he arose and dressed, it was with a new energy, as if he had slept peacefully for a long time. She had breakfast ready for him in the kitchen, two eggs with buttered toast and American coffee. They did not kiss when he left for work. It was not that kind of goodbye; but when he stood up from the table to put on his coat, Navabi let his hand return momentarily to her waist and then, at a final word, to caress her hip the way a husband would do.

Once outside he faced the frozen accumulation of the night and made his way to the road with difficulty. There was a long walk ahead of him, and Navabi was unfamiliar with crusted snow and tire troughs in the street. He found it harder to walk in compacted places, almost falling to his knees several times. Because there were no sidewalk to make the going easier, he felt that he had already worked a full shift after he'd struggled a block or two. His thoughts went to Tomás trying to forge his way from the slippery porch to the corner where his school bus would stop. Then he wondered if the schools would be open at all. One of the many rules and customs that he still did not understand. After another half block Navabi heard the crunch of tires some distance behind him.

He turned to notice a long black vehicle making its way down the street. For a moment it paused at Fabiana's house and then crept forward until it came alongside him. The passenger side window went down, and someone said, "Mr. Kolchak!"

The person was speaking to him.

"Mr. Kolchak, get in. I have some good news!"

Navabi stamped the snow from his shoes and got into the car. The window went up, sealing him uncomfortably in the sudden warmth. "It's cold out there, isn't it?" offered Mrs. Leonitis.

"Yes, it is very cold," said Navabi.

"I thought it was you, walking along there. Where are you headed?"

"The mill," he said. "I work at the mill."

"The mill, that's right. I remember now. Give you a lift. I've got an appointment in that direction."

"Thank you."

Mrs. Leonitis looked at him and smiled. "I hate driving in this mess. I bet you hate walking in it too."

Something cold and hazy, like one of the snow clouds, began to gather in Mr. Navabi's abdomen. "You said you had news."

"Oh. Yes. Your family. Your old family I mean. They've been approved! They'll be going to Seattle. Isn't that great?"

The words came to him like an echo from a well. Just noise at first and then, gradually, meaning. *Kameela, Sabir, Nalani.* They had been approved. A stroke of good fortune, he assumed. He had to take the woman's word for it, but the news unbalanced him. Navabi could not summon the proper words. Finally he simply repeated, "Yes. That would be great." He did not know Seattle or how far it might be from this frozen world.

Mrs. Leonitis continued talking and steering the car into the ruts made by previous cars. Mr. Navabi, the new Richard, wondered if there had been other new Richards before the worn out one that he himself had replaced. He assumed so. But instead of asking about Seattle, he asked, "What will happen next? To them, I mean."

And, remarkably, Mrs. Leonitis knew what he meant. "Fabiana? The children? They'll be moving," she told him. "To someplace nice." Then after another minute she went on, "Or, I suppose, you could keep things as they are. Your choice really. Your choice." She tilted her head and looked at him.

In America, they had told him, making a new life was as easy as opening one door and closing another. And now, only moments after awakening to Fabiana, this. *I have come from so very far away* he thought. The car bumped and veered as if steering no longer mattered, only momentum. Navabi imagined himself back in Lebanon, making promises that he could not keep.

"Your choice," prompted Mrs. Leonitis. The voice of America it seemed. And only a mild curiosity that now preceded the proper forms being filled out.

Mr. Navabi heard himself saying, "Seattle. I want you to move me to Seattle" with a kind of finality that mystified him. The words sounded faint and remote, and he wondered if Mrs. Leonitis was surprised as well. But she seemed unmoved, her eyes fixed on the road ahead.

The car crept forward another quarter mile and then stopped at the next intersection. Navabi opened the door, stepped out into the cold, and then continued toward the mill where he was known as a very good worker and a friend to many who labored there.

JAMES CONOR PATTERSON

the property bubble

love. let's try on this life like a rented tux.
adapt to the driveway scattered with motor oil
& tire tracks left by some errant cement truck.
let's keep the charade until the suit is soiled;
stuffed—one in each leg—like some ersatz
laurel & hardy into the same pair of slacks.
someday these houses will be carved into flats
but for now let's enjoy the fruits of our stamp tax:
the sound of knotweed climbing the stairs,
the moon framed in a punched-out window,
cinder-block walls gone fat with prayers
& somewhere, the nightman's diminuendo.
let's make a life here when equity's ours.
when ireland is free. when man steps on mars.

alien big cat

pretty soon that two-bit wholesaler's spanish revival villa was a distant memory & only the verdant grey of the carnbane townland stood between me & an approximation of freedom. i avoided the whistling dart from the handler's gun for two whole weeks. could almost see the smug bastard's face plastered over *BBC newsline* talking about police helicopters & "specialist" sniffer dogs. his nasal whinny superseded only by the bright rosacea broken across his nose. his idiot grin the rictus of an overly satisfied wolf. i'd rather spend my mornings tramping through the marshes. would rather the cage in that coke dealer's garage—diesel tanks hung like andean crags—than the chirp of some bird in that charity mugger's bunker . . . i've to hand it to him—the dealer—he had *taste*, for mine wasn't the only rump in that locked menagerie. here were tigers & pygmy hippos, parrots & green anacondas; gifts from some big dick in rural colombia who'd picked us like fruit for the curation of a welcome. i was to be the jewel in his smallman's crown; that *rare melanistic leopard* they've been talking about these weeks. these irish. if only i had eyes, i'd roll them back in my head.

STEPHANIE CHOI

Lipogram

This poem will not be a lipogram.

The following sentence will try to explain what happened without the letter e:

In my youth I got a tattoo with a word that's missing an __.

This poem is not inspired by the novel *Gadsby*, whose cover touts it as a 50,000-word novel without the letter e.

This poem is not inspired by the book *La Disparition*, inspired by the book *Gadsby*.

This poem is not inspired.

What happened is that when I was twenty I got a tattoo from a guy my friend met at a club.

What happened is that my friend met a guy at a club who said he *did tattoos* and exchanged Snapchats with him.

What happened is that we tapped through his artist portfolio, made up of photos that disappeared after five seconds.

What happened is that my friend wanted a pinecone and I wanted a tree with some lines from a poem I loved.

What happened is that he quoted us a quarter of studio prices and arrived at her house with his toolbox full of needles and ink.

What happened is that I was twenty.

What happened is that he plastic wrapped the kitchen table and for three hours I clutched my friend's couch pillow.

What happened is that he misspelled the word _____.

What happened is that he said *sometimes it can be painful on the back . . . over the spine.*

What happened is that I already knew pain in my spine.

What happened is a childhood diagnosis, an adolescent correction.

What happened is that I wore a back brace and then I didn't.

What happened is that I hid the brace under a revolving trove of various large, plain colored T-shirts I made my mother buy for me from the craft store.

What happened made invisible.

What happened is that when I stopped wearing the brace the pain remained.

What happened is that the pain from the needles would at least leave something visible.

What happened is that because "e" is the most common letter, it's often mis-seen—the mind places it there, where it is not.

What happened is that I mis-saw.

What happened is that it was not an intentional omission of the letter "e," but a mistake.

What happened is that a friend finally noticed and said *I'm so sorry to tell you this.*

What happened is that the word *loneliness* is missing its first "e."

What happened is that I took it as a sign.

What happened is that I was twenty and desired *meaning.*

What happened is that the word loneliness went from long to short O.

What happened is that the tattoo is on my back, which means I never see it.

What happened is that the tattoo is on my back, which means I always see it:

A tattoo with a word missing an __, and I with a story.

RHETT ISEMAN TRULL

Music Box

When I let myself in, my brother is singing, up
in his room where he thinks he's alone. As if
to a safe unlocking, I tune my ear, as if now might be revealed
secrets known only to the pinball wizard, jack sprung
from a box, and carousel ponies the moment the ride
switches on. All summer, he's hidden
his voice, no matter how I begged for
just one song. Is his refusal
vengeance for that hide-and-seek, long ago,
when I let the neighbor girls convince me
to abdicate my role as It, though Jim alone remained to find
and would remain, tucked behind the holly,
as its leaves performed their cruelty on his skin
and the sun dropped toward the spiny curtain
of the trees and his sister was not coming, was not even looking, was
in the basement watching MTV, trying to be like the older girls.
I wish he'd remember instead how we found each other
other times, when storms would out the lights
or the algae eater we loved—strange against the glass—
went belly up in the greening tank; or how, when he was little
and wanted it opened and closed, opened and closed, I'd
bring my music box down from the high shelf,
though I feared he might break it.

More likely, he remembers his first solo, his
Winthrop who'd barely speak until that wagon with its
promised trumpet was on its way, his opening night, night I ran
from the theater, disappeared again, might have been
thinking suicide for all he knew, couldn't explain
those dark halls inside me lit by music. Is he, too,
unable to separate the two events, the two of us?
Or does he think of me at all anymore? And
which is worse? A month from now,

he'll make his one exception—or so he thinks—to this
summer's silence, at Tony's, the beach's
lone Italian fine dining, where he'll stop busing tables, turn
to surprise us: his *happy birthday to you* to our mother, a cappella,
laying down every spaghetti-twisted fork, pulling even
the cooks from the kitchen. He's that good.

I've wondered if he fears the presence of an audience
dilutes, somehow, the instrument. But
walking in on him tonight, I understand: he's
Orpheus, dangerous power to move a stone, to make

and unmake, incite to further madness those
already unhinged, inspire the gods
to call Eurydice out of the dark. I wish
I could tell him it's not his fault his song
becomes mine when I hear it.
The roof is lifting off the scaffold of this house.
Knives in their drawers have gone percussive.
My brother's song is sky at dusk unfolding its stars, galoshes
troubling a puddle back to rain. It's the old
strange tremble in my chest when, to prove it wasn't
the quick kind, I stepped out onto the sand to learn it was.

I dare not stir, not even to slip the keys
to the counter. I am next to enter
the coliseum: *we who are about to die,* next
to be fired from the cannon, next soul
for whom the gate with its pearls like teeth
has opened. The boat tacks now toward
our new country. Words drop from our tongues
like tickets, spent. One day scholars writing *A History of Language*
will sink their heads to their desks, stumped
by the lost word *brother.* Hold on. He

slows it down, wraps each note in a softness, opposite
of mussels in their shells. I remember myself, farther back.
Unlike the flimsy ballerina in the music box, turning
over and over over the years to her one song, I've been spun
by many, all part of the same: cheap kazoo prize

from the Guess Your Age booth, tobacco-clouded
codger every autumn bringing our piano
into tune, Mama humming at the end
of a set of lullabies she rocked me nightly to
while my brother slept inside her waiting to be born.

JAMES BRUNTON

Queer History

I am reading about history
figured here as a word
in quotation marks or crossed out to indicate
the rejection of the idea of progress.

I look up at irregular intervals, searching
the white sky, backlit and blinding,
like looking into the past.

I think it is worth remembering
the ties you've cut and why, the events
that make you the kind of person

who goes rigid when embraced,
worth mentioning, maybe, to someone
younger and wise with the weight

of our immense present,
the historical repetitions keeping us
generationally on edge.

Call it progress: a series of names—
epithet, movement, chosen—
or narratives constructed in therapists' offices

or in someone else's bed, far from home.
Our time is limited. When I return
to the page it is to tell you

a history of the rejection of ideas.

MELISSA KWASNY

The Apple Tree in Blossom

functions like a windbreak a deer disappears into
or a conversation wherein the point is lost.
A dressing room for the angels to try on
their various costumes: a swarm of mosquitos,
a net of light that snags the bunting's flimsy song.
I am rapidly disappearing into the numerous,
and into shyness. Oh, the scholar I tried to be!
I am eating white petals from a voluptuous,
rose-like sea, as if it had any ceremonial purpose.
A dog barks all day on a very short chain.
Lengthen the chain and the world has hope again.
My friend has Alzheimer's. Here, give this
almond to the dog, I say, and she nods and chews it.
My friend is a changing situation. She wanders
her old routes through the gardens, staring at what
she will no longer be able to find. That part
of your life is over, we could each say, at any point,
which is terrible and sad, intimacy being
a better goal than non-attachment. The apple tree
is old, almost sixty-five years, its trunk bent
under its loft. Loft, a tender word, as in the past
tense of lift. Loft, as the measure of the fluffiness
of down. Aloft. Afloat. Aflutter. A calm.
Someone planted it knowing it would outlast them.

A "FIELD" SYMPOSIUM

on

Reginald Shepherd

edited by
Jericho Brown & Kevin Prufer

Introduction

When *Field* magazine closed shop after an astonishing 50 years of service to the world of poetry, editors Martha Collins, David Walker, and David Young gave *Copper Nickel* permission to adopt *Field*'s Symposium format for our pages. As ever, we are deeply grateful for that permission.

For those who aren't familiar, each of *Field*'s Symposia focused on one specific poet. The editors would recruit several contemporary poets each to pick a single poem by the poet-of-focus and to write a brief essay explaining why the poem they chose is excellent (what's unique about it, what makes it tick, why it moves them, etc.). The poems were then reprinted alongside the essays—and, thus, the resulting five decades of Symposia offered personalized, multifaceted representations and appreciations of dozens of important and exciting poets.

For our purposes at *Copper Nickel*, the "Field" Symposium format offers us the possibility to do similar work for deceased writers we believe are undervalued and/or at risk of being forgotten. Our first Symposium, co-edited by Piotr Florczyk, was in issue 33 (fall 2021) and focused on the Irish poet, novelist, and essayist Ciaran Carson, who died in 2019.

This second Symposium focuses on the singular, iconoclastic, and brilliant poet Reginald Shepherd, who died of cancer in 2008 at the age of 45. By the time of his death, Shepherd had published five poetry collections (and a sixth would come out posthumously). He had also written two books of criticism and had edited two anthologies—each of which advocates for a combination of high lyricism, aesthetic openness, hybridity, and experiment. In his critical books, Shepherd articulates a nuanced skepticism toward emphasizing "identity" in poetry, but he's also very clear about who he was: a Black, gay poet who was raised in poverty and instability, and who—as he explains in an interview in the spring 1998 issue of *Callaloo*—sought to "replace or overwrite" his "identity as a poor person" with the identity of "Artist." His poems—as you will find in the selection in this Symposium—are concentrated lyrics full of sharp imagery, rhythmic language, and a highly crafted musicality. And Shepherd was always profoundly conscious of the many ways his writing could both extend and complicate poetic tradition.

The Selected Shepherd, edited by Jericho Brown, will be published in April 2024 by the University of Pittsburgh Press. The fact that *The Selected Shepherd* was in production led *Copper Nickel* Contributing Editor Kevin Prufer and the *Copper Nickel* staff to start thinking about the possiblity of a Symposium on Shepherd, which could help draw attention to Shepherd's work generally, and to the forthcoming book specifically. Prufer and *Copper Nickel* invited Brown to co-edit the feature, and he quickly agreed.

At that point, Brown and Prufer began contacting poets who had, at one moment or another, expressed an overt interest in Shepherd's work. Soon seven poets had agreed to contribute: Rick Barot, Tommye Blount, Timothy Liu, Lama Rod Owens, Camille Rankine, Paisley Rekdal, and Charles Stephens. We at *Copper Nickel* are grateful for their contributions and for Brown and Prufer's dedicated editorial work. We're also grateful to the University of Pittsburgh Press for allowing us to reprint the seven poems by Shepherd included in the feature.

If you're already familiar with Shepherd's work, we hope the essays offer new insights. If you're not familiar with Shepherd's work, we hope this Symposium offers an exciting and enduring discovery.

———————

Books by Reginald Shepherd:

POETRY COLLECTIONS

Some Are Drowning (1994)

Angel, Interrupted (1996)

Wrong (1999)

Otherhood (2003)

Fata Morgana (2007)

Red Clay Weather (2011)

CRITICISM

Orpheus in the Bronx: Essays on Identity, Politics, and the Freedom of Poetry (2008)

A Martian Muse: Further Readings on Identity, Politics, and the Freedom of Poetry (2010)

EDITED ANTHOLOGIES

The Iowa Anthology of New American Poetries (2004)

Lyric Postmodernisms (2008)

Self-Portrait as First Snow

Every perspective fails, blotted in blank mist
that smothers all proportion, three seasons heaped
under sleep. How I would like to sleep,
but I would miss your rising drifts
arriving out my fogged-in window. I woke to winter
falling safely down the pane, flat backdrop of storm
daylight recedes into, gray with a coin of white
where the sun should be. On afternoons like this
how featureless the day's one face becomes. How pale
you have become, how much you'd like to fade
into the cloud-filled dusk: it smooths away
your face, proposes you a tree frosted with ice
against a clearing nightfall, a snowflake's
perfect sphere beside the half-inflated moon.

Reading Shepherd

Rick Barot

A BLIZZARD AFTERNOON IN NEW York City in the mid 1990s. I still remember the first time I read Reginald Shepherd's first book, *Some Are Drowning*, and my feeling, as the afternoon and the snow deepened, that I had been given another dimension of my own privacy. I remember reading one poem after another and looking up to my own reflected face in the window, hazy with love, hurt, dream—the things in Shepherd's poems that seemed to see me and enlarge me.

The search for one's own face: a poet tries on masks, tries on voices, calls upon all the technical and thematic catalysts at hand, calls upon the imagination, calls upon the real, to apprehend that face. I don't mean the face of flesh that gleams and ages through time, though this face and its fate keenly play into the poet's search. I mean the face of the supposed person that Dickinson proposed: not the poet herself, but the person in the poems who enacts her surges of thought and feeling. The face that is consciousness manifested, with the complexities of interiority given a legible and warm surface. This is the face that is the subject of Shepherd's "Self-Portrait as First Snow," one of the poems I keep returning to, over these many decades, in *Some Are Drowning*.

Even if it contains no explicit autobiographical material, every poem is a self portrait. And when a poet writes a poem that's announced as a self-portrait, they acknowledge the notion that the self is always the subject after all. In the first sentence of Shepherd's poem, what's moving about the gaze on the self is the admission that the gaze begins in failure, that the enterprise of looking is motivated by uncertainty. A disorientation, an ache, a mystery: a poem begins there. In "Self-Portrait," the source of uncertainty is ostensibly the snowy atmosphere that the speaker is in, but "perspective" also alerts us to the possibility that more than one kind of perceiving is being obscured. The simultaneity is made more so by the invocation of "three seasons heaped / under sleep." The three seasons might refer to the seasons prior to winter, or to a metaphoric set of seasons lived by the speaker. What those seasons contained, we don't know, but as suggested by "fails," "blotted," "smothers," and "heaped," the dark weight of those seasons is what the first sentence carries.

"How I would like to sleep," the second sentence of "Self-Portrait" intones, "but I would miss your rising drifts / arriving out my fogged-in window." In that direct address to the snowfall, Shepherd points to the longing, part grief and part eros, that runs through his poems. If Shepherd is anything he is a love poet, though the epithet simplifies what are various and complicated forms of desire and vision in his poetry. He looks at the landscape and the urbanscape. He looks at the painting. He looks at myths, the gods and their victims. He looks at the shirtless boy in the park. The erotic is present in all of them. And in that gap between the gazer and the object, one recourse of the speaker is to address the you, in a gesture of intimacy that only highlights the object's inability or unwillingness to hear. In "Self-Portrait," to address the snowfall is to give it the scale of the personal, the snow's ungovernable drifts made to fit into the size of the speaker's window.

The final sentence of "Self-Portrait as First Snow" is once again a turn to a you, but not the earlier you of the snowfall, but the you of the self: "How pale / you have become, how much you'd like to fade / into the cloud-filled dusk." Reading these lines, I go back to the obsessed absorption I felt with Shepherd's work all through the 1990s. I was still new to writing poems, and "Self-Portrait" seemed to describe the poet in me—a gaunt, romantically pale figure. The desire "to fade / into the cloud-filled dusk" seemed to echo the speaker's statement in Keats's "Ode to a Nightingale" that "I have been half in love with easeful Death," and also the desperate conclusion of his "Bright star" sonnet: "And so live ever—or else swoon to death." In his wish to dissolve, Shepherd's speaker was updating Keats's swoon. In that way, Shepherd was familiar because he was clearly in dialogue with the poets I loved then. Even his use of the sonnet—signaled by the *abba* rhyme scheme of the first four lines, then blithely dropped in the rest of the poem—was another instance of Shepherd's recognizable affinities as a poet.

In "Self-Portrait," the speaker's paleness is only one instance of the mystique that whiteness has in Shepherd's poems. White bodies, white weather—tropes of whiteness appear in his work as erotic and intellectual motifs. Shepherd reckons with race and racism in his poetry, but poetry, for him, was not necessarily meant for what he called "political efficacy." If poetry was political, it was only as a place where a vivid contemporary multiplicity could be captured. "In my work," Shepherd writes in an essay, "I wish to make Sappho and the South Bronx, the myth of Hyacinth and the homeless black men ubiquitous in the cities of the decaying American empire, AIDS and all the beautiful, dead cultures, speak to and acknowledge one another." This wish manifests as gorgeous artifice and brooding vision in his poems. One of the primary tensions in Shepherd's work is between his love of transcendent beauty and the inescapable traumas of his social and political self.

One of Shepherd's earliest poems, "Self-Portrait as First Snow" is a statement of poetics as well as a self-portrait. Shepherd's sensibility and vision are packed richly into the poem, particularly his belief in poetry as a catalyst for transformation. "My self was always too much with me," Shepherd writes in an essay, adding, "My search wasn't for identity but for a way out of identity, out of those shackles of selfhood I'd never chosen." In the last lines of "Self-Portrait," when the speaker wishes to fade into the snow-soft dusk, he also imagines the moment past that fading, when the self is brought to figurative intensity. The dusk is not oblivion. Instead, it is a kind of tenderness.

The Gods at Three A.M.

The foolish gods are doing poppers while they sing along,
they're taking off their white T-shirts and wiping the sweat
from their foreheads with them, the gods have tattoos
of skulls and roses on their shoulders, perhaps a pink triangle
above the left nipple, for them there's hope. The gods
are pausing to light cigarettes while they dance, they're laughing
at private jokes while the smoke machine comes on,
one of the gods told you they put talcum powder
in the artificial fog, then walked away, how could anyone
breathe talcum powder, but it makes their skin shine
with the sweat and smell of cigarettes and Obsession. Don't try
to say you didn't know the gods are always white, the statues
told you that. The gods don't say hello, and when you ask them
how they are the gods say they don't know, the gods
are drunk and don't feel like talking now, but you
can touch their muscled backs when they pass.

The gods in backwards baseball caps say
free love, they say *this is the time*, and disappear
into another corner of the bar, they're always moving
to another song. The gods with their checked flannel
shirts unbuttoned under open motorcycle jackets,
hard nipples and ghost-white briefs above the waistbands
of their baggy jeans, say *get here*, the gods say *soon*, and you just
keep dancing because you don't know the words, you hope
the gods will notice small devotions and smile, maybe
a quick thumbs-up if you're good. The gods
whose perfect instances of bodies last only
for the instant, or until last call (and then
they disappear into the sidewalk), gods who are splendid
without meaning to be, who do they need
to impress, say *this could be the magic*, they say
live for tonight, and then the lights come on.

Getting Free from the Gods at Three A.M.

Lama Rod Owens

I FIRST MET REGINALD IN 2001, during my senior year at Berry College when he visited the campus to give a reading and work with a cohort of student poets of which I was a member. He was Black and gay, the two things I especially hated about myself back then. On top of that he was confident, unapologetically talented, and unphased by how the world was attempting to erase men like us. His boldness scared me. He was a mirror reflecting to me everything I was trying to repress because I thought repression was how we survived anti-Black and queerphobic spaces. In a way, I did not want to see him. I both hated and loved him and resented myself for getting lost in the tension. However, within the first 30 minutes of his arrival on campus, I became a moth drawn to his light and catching him alone, I shyly confessed: "I read your essay in *In the Life*. Thank you." He paused, then smiled slowly as if amused that anyone here on a campus with almost no diversity would even know that book let alone link him to it. "Yeah," he finally responded chuckling, "that was a while ago."

He'd arrived during a particularly difficult period for me. He knew this and attempted to connect with me more during his short visit. I appreciated the effort. After his visit, we exchanged a few emails, but I didn't allow myself to open to his care and concern. I wanted to keep my pain to myself.

Eventually, I would train to become a lama or teacher in the Tibetan tradition of Buddhism. My training supported a deep healing as well as a remembrance of so many who had reached out to help over my healing journey. And when I was finally ready to reconnect with him to offer my appreciation for his care, he had already left us, becoming an ancestor.

I have read and studied most of Reginald's work for over 20 years now. He believed that poetry was about the possibility of who we could be, not necessarily who we were in this moment. I don't believe that this was an expression of shame, but rather an acknowledgment that we could be and are much more than we think we are. I loved Reginald not because he was the first poet to tell them this, but because he was the first poet who I believed.

"The Gods at Three A.M." has been a poem that has lived with me for years now. The poem is set in a club or bar. The scene is familiar. The space crowded by "foolish gods," white men, some bare chested, tattooed, dripping with sweat. They are laughing, cigarette smoke along with a smoke machine blowing talcum powder hovered thick in the space. Imagine the music; something belted by one of our favorite divas or the heavy sweat rhythm of house music— something that the body can lose itself in. And there is the speaker, maybe standing in a corner or by a back wall, gazing out into the space.

All this is familiar because I have been this speaker. The poem is my voice, echoes my thoughts, pronounces my desire. I've been in that club longing for the attention of white men because white supremacist conditioning has rendered me longing for something other than myself, longing for gods or the mythic sacredness of white men, not because they necessarily love me or would make ideal partners, but because I have been taught not to long for men who look like me.

When I met Reginald, I felt ugly and believed that beauty was for the gods until I realized that the experience of beauty, like many things, has been colonized and thus weaponized against me as yet another thing that I do not have access to. But this has been the influence of Reginald's work and care on me, reminding me that beauty isn't gatekept by pretty white boys but is an expression of love for myself and the right to claim my own beauty. Beauty is my inherent belief that I am beautiful, and my beauty relies on the love I have for myself, not through the validation of others.

However, this poem is about more than the longing for white men's bodies or the desire for my beauty to be validated. It is also a poignant reminder that even these gods do not endure.

In Buddhism, there are mythologies of different realms of beings. Two of these realms are the human realm and the God's realm. We abide in the human, an existence of bodies and desire, living and dying, but endowed with the mental and spiritual capacities to free ourselves from this cycle of birth and rebirth to achieve a state free from suffering.

The Gods are beings born from immense good merit into an existence of pleasure, long lives, and a bypassing of pain and suffering. But things always end for the Gods because their perpetual state of bliss cannot be sustained forever as suffering is meant to be faced, metabolized, and released, to allow our hearts to break in the breaking remind us that real sustainable joy is rooted in letting go of the fear of experiencing suffering. Suffering is only an experience where awareness and care have not yet learned to be tended to.

The God's realm can also be a mental state. In life, we find ourselves in the god's realm anytime we get stuck in pleasure while vehemently avoiding suffering. As we learn in the poem, the lights will come on, the gods will stumble back into the world only to remember they cannot endure, that they will "disappear into the sidewalk."

This poem lives so closely with me because it reminds me that real joy and even freedom begin when I first start to want myself. It's not that I need to give up all desire for white men or the need for any validation from others. I just need to be the one I want first so my desire for other men is held first in a poignant confidence in my own desirability and beauty. I wish I could tell Reginald how much he has been a part of this healing. However, it seems like I just did.

Paradise

I don't know the names of flowers, or the various
songs of birds, what to call the water
falling from the sky all week, sleet or hail,
the histories of high achievement while my
great-grandparents were hidden among the cotton,
slaves. (I know what to call asphalt
slick with rain, but not the parts of that plant
that shredded their fingers.) *Thou bringest home
all things day scattered*, but let the lost, this once,
bury the lost. So much stolen that was free
for the asking. . . . Let the mutilated days sort out
their own. Swallow, swallow, when shall I
be like the swallow, singing the rape
of my voice, but singing past the rape, something
my own to sing? And not to live by white men's
myths (not to reject those too-clear eyes, but not
to long for them, or see through their blue distances
all colors but my own), or drown in that exhaustion
of hyacinth and narcissus mown down. I don't know
names of flowers, though I can mimic
those who do, the open secret of a man
who doesn't look like me, who looks like me
if I could speak my name, if I could stop
the repetitions of oppressive beauties
not my own. (I don't trust beauty anymore,
when will I stop believing it?) Skylark, I don't know
if you can find that paradise, or lead me to
the blackened ruins of my song.

Something My Own to Sing:
On Reginald Shepherd's "Paradise"

Camille Rankine

WHEN I CAME ACROSS THE opening lines of Reginald Shepherd's poem "Paradise," I felt an immediate connection. I was re-engaging with his work in preparation for an event to be held in his memory, where I had been invited to read one of his poems. It was 2009, and I had just completed an MFA at Columbia, where I'd often felt a bit like an imposter, as if I didn't have the right language, the correct set of references to make a poem. I didn't know the names of flowers, either.

At its opening, "Paradise" pits the urban against the natural. Shepherd aligns himself with the former. I imagine Shepherd, or a version of him, as this poem's speaker: the voice feels intimate and undeniably connected with the practice of poem making. Knowledge of the natural world, we discover, belongs to his great-grandparents, who picked cotton as slaves. Shepherd knows "what to call asphalt / slick with rain, but not the part of that plant / that shredded their fingers." For me, this was the poem's first surprise in a series of surprises. I thought the poem meant to indicate that knowledge of flowers and birds belonged to the pastoral world of the established poetry canon—a traditionally white space—whereas Blackness existed in the cultural imagination as the product of an urban environment. Here, Shepherd gives Blackness back its claim to the earth. That connection to the natural world is reframed as something that might have been his once, but is now lost. "Let the lost, this once, / bury the lost," he continues—after quoting a fragment of Sappho. Another surprise. The poem at once turning away from and laying claim to the language and references we understand as classically poetic, while, at the same time, both claiming and turning away from the grief and grievances of the past.

"In my work I wish to make Sappho and the South Bronx, the myth of Hyacinth and the homeless black men ubiquitous in the cities of the decaying American empire, AIDS and all the beautiful, dead cultures, speak to and acknowledge one another," writes Shepherd, in an essay from his book *Orpheus in the Bronx.*

In "Paradise," I see these different worlds in conversation. Sappho is here, and hyacinth, too:

> And not to live by white men's
> myths (not to reject those too-clear eyes, but not
> to long for them, or see through their blue distances

all colors but my own), or drown in that exhaustion
of hyacinth and narcissus mown down.

Hyacinth and narcissus appear here in lowercase, as flowers he apparently *does* know the name of. Surprise. But their appearance together inevitably calls them forward as myth, as does the reference to "white men's myths" a few lines earlier. In these lines, I see those opposing impulses again, the turning both toward and away—a recognition of the allure of whiteness and its aesthetic, coupled with suspicion, a mistrust of its "oppressive beauties," as he says later, and the way it threatens to limit his voice, his vision of the world and himself. For me, this scrutiny of whiteness was another of the poem's surprises.

I first encountered Reginald Shepherd as a student. It was maybe 2006, and he was visiting Columbia to give a talk on craft. In my memory, he focused on his frustration with the construct of identity in poetry, the idea that as a Black, gay poet, his poems should necessarily be expressive of these aspects of his identity, and be read strictly through that lens. As he spoke, I felt as if he was giving language to my own quiet anxieties about my work, my fear that preconceived notions of my Blackness would overwrite my words and render my poetry illegible.

I carried this anxiety for years. But as I grew and evolved as a poet, so did my relationship to my identity on the page, and my ideas about the ways that identity and artistic expression intertwine. Today, reading Shepherd's arguments about identity poetics—that this mode limits possibility, paints the poet into a socially constructed corner, where the only thing they express is a performative Black self—I often find myself arguing aloud with his words.

Returning to his poetry, to "Paradise," I see the complexity of Shepherd's relationship to identity (and its poetics) unfold in its lines, the push and pull of their movement. "I don't know / the names of flowers, though I can mimic / those who do," Shepherd says, toward the poem's close. Is this poem an example of that mimicry? Its hyacinth and narcissus a costume of poetic legitimacy? It's as if, within the poem, the poet questions himself, his own authenticity. This uncertainty appeals to me. The poem thinking through the problem of itself. It doesn't make an argument, it is *in* argument. A discourse that remains unresolved, ending, essentially, on the admission, "I don't know."

That "I don't know" pulls me back toward what I see as the poem's central question, its center of gravity: "When shall I / be like the swallow, singing the rape / of my voice, but singing past the rape, something / my own to sing?" At the same time, it propels me toward the final plea: "lead me to / the blackened ruins of my song." This movement, looping backward to a ruined past, recalls the poem's opening, which brought us back to a time when the natural world was the domain of Blackness, of Shepherd's enslaved forebears, not just the lofty terrain of the poet.

In hoping to sing past the rape of his voice, he also seeks to travel back to a time before that rape, that lost place a mirror of the paradise beyond, both spaces where he might make a music unquestionably his own.

I wonder, did he reach that paradise? I don't mean in death, though perhaps I mean that, too. But did his poems find that song of his own to sing? If I listen to the words he's left behind, I would say that goal may be unattainable, "an asymptote toward which one strives, at which one never arrives." What we have, instead, is the beauty of his efforts toward it.

The Friend

This recurring dream after the lethargies
of listless reading, restless wanderings
through books that always seem posthumous,
words another might have read
with profit, falling from the hand like tattered leaves
the trees cast off, picked up and scattered
on a casual walk, blank pages shredded as snow
that mounts against the window he raps on.
How does he know my name when I am so often another
in the dream? This body isn't mine, but takes me travelling
when it moves. There, I am only the ghost
who starts the play, attendant on my spectacle.
He wants to be like that, the absent
omnipresent one; he wants to be the blood-red moon
and not the startled children pointing. Nothing
startles him; he wants it to inherit me.

In the dream I am always posthumous,
the sole survivor of myself
in the rubble of my city soaked in soldiers
and fine-grained mist. *That's my brother,*
he lies, and leaves me with a photograph of snow.
As if it were a photograph of me. One is anywhere
in the dream. So that's where I wait, and of course he is there,
invisible as always, a doorway as always,
with the fear that nothing comes to an end.
He wants to do everything just once, he sleeps
eyes open. *So I won't miss it when it comes back. So it won't be
the same.* He plays a game with clouds and calls it swimming,
washes ashore as the world. Made of the singular. Made of
the blanks. The one standing at the half-open door
with a familiar shape, the one in bed who can't move.
Who is it, I ask, but he won't tell me his name.

On Reginald Shepherd's "The Friend"

Timothy Liu

I met Reginald Shepherd on the page in the early Nineties before his first book, *Some Are Drowning*, was published. Those were the days before anything online, when you hung out in the stacks of the university library (or magazine racks at the local literary bookstore) to get a pulse of what was being published right then and there, ambitious to get your own poems (and name) out into the world. *Other* names kept popping up—Bob Hicok, Reginald Shepherd, Virgil Suarez. In those days, you had to ask around to find out more about who these faceless names were, no internet searches or email addresses available. It was mostly snail mail or nada. I must have read dozens of Reginald Shepherd poems over the years before ever reaching out.

•

It was probably sometime after our second books found their way into print that we both ended up having *email* addresses. Back in those days, no one had cell phones. Some folks had *pagers* (my first boyfriend in Houston was an EMT). We all had *land lines* and long-distance providers like MCI (a monthly $400 bill was not an uncommon sight, and on my grad-school budget, a real killer!). My first encounters with Reginald: a few emails followed by mostly phone calls. We were almost always attached to some institution of higher education, as students and/or teachers. What did we talk about? Mostly other poets, what we had been reading, whom we had encountered, bitching about terrible poets landing poems in great places and receiving undeserved accolades, that sort of thing. And boy oh boy, did we dig in about the poets we had *studied* with!

•

I suppose there was a healthy amount of competition between us, but it was never about the *poems*, more about the *places*, the attention, and the *gatekeepers*. Our poems didn't *sound* like each other's even though we were both queer writers of color, and in those days, that meant more trailblazing opportunities than it does today. We found refuge under the same covers when the gatekeepers were hospitable (Marilyn Hacker at *Kenyon Review* or Richard Howard at *Paris Review* come to mind). Poems full of cock and cum and HIV were harder to land in prestigious journals, the homosexual and homoerotic largely seen as indecorous, even suspect. I suppose it remains so today as I continue castrating some of my poems of racy diction, mopping up the syntactical fluids to make them what, more presentable? Reginald loved my line "ass meat spread in centerfolds a canine wrenches free," which found its way into the pages of *Sulfur*.

•

Which brings me to "The Friend" which landed in the hallowed pages of *Poetry* more than thirty years ago where many of Reginald's poems would find their future home, sometimes crowned with a prize there! Even before his first book, I don't know if Reginald thought he would live long, into old age, more identified with Keats than Wordsworth. The word "posthumous" in "The Friend" is a dead ringer. He had survived the Bronx, the projects, had matriculated at MFA writing programs at Brown *and* Iowa (so much for the notion of a *terminal* degree). Like many without a first book, we went to any school that gave us the moola so we could keep on writing without having to take too many dumb jobs to support an ultimately unsustainable habit. We all knew that without significant publications, the degree was good for nothing but to wipe your ass meat with.

•

I like Reginald's use of pronouns in "The Friend." The tango of the "I" and the "He" reminds me of a poem like Ashbery's "My Erotic Double." This kind of doubling (and double consciousness) is amplified by the "recurring dream" template that overlays the proceedings, this realm of an eroticized in-between that straddles the body/mind, black/white, art/life and love/death divides. In this poem, with "blank pages shredded as snow" and the narrator being left "with a photograph of snow," we become aware not only of the preserve of art but its erasures, how whiteness can serve as a kind of correction fluid for Blackness (or anything queer multiculti). If you conducted a search in all of Reginald's books of poems for terms like "white," "black" and "body," you would discover some unmistakable patterns. I like the construction of "The Friend"—two neat sixteen-line end-stopped stanzas, almost as contained as a double sonnet, but spilling over. The poem would also work as eight quatrains, so tight and masterful as its line breaks are. But the two-stanza format makes rhetorical sense.

•

Reginald was a friend. Neither of us were huge *fans* of each other's poems, but we showed each other a good amount of respect. Respectful platonic distance mixed with irreverent candor is one way I would put it. We both had white boyfriends. One thing we talked about more than poetry was opera, particularly opera recordings. His obsession ran deep and bottomless. He particularly relished the *Sturm und Drang* of Wagnerian extremity. Whose Brünhilde mattered more, Eva Marton's or Hildegard Behrens'? What was it about Anja Silja's Senta that put her above the rest? Could Waltraud Meier really hold a candle to Flagstad's Isolde? Maybe in every poetic friendship, there has to be something extra-poetic that can serve as the glue in order to give Poesy a needed and deserved rest.

•

The Beloved Friend is "the one standing at the half-open door / with a familiar shape" and "the one in bed who can't move." Erect and supine. Familiar and strange. Mobile and locked down. Robust and ill. Reginald died of complications from liver cancer as he battled HIV/AIDS in the last decade of his life. The betrayals of the body consecrated his mind, his mythic art. He found solace in the operatic, high and low cultures inextricably conjoined, the Boystown of Halsted a stone's throw from Chicago's Lyric Opera House if David were Goliath or vice versa. Reginald was loyal to his closest poet friends; they are acknowledged in all of his books. Reginald spoke his mind, made enemies wherever he went. He was the epitome of being uncompromising, and he paid the social price, lost opportunities and jobs. Can't you feel it in this poem, his act of self-prophecy? He couldn't *help* himself. Perhaps the source of all his genius.

The Lucky One

The middle-aged white man in a beat-up blue Pinto
who shouts "Hey man, what's up?", pulls up onto
the curb in front of me to ask the time, because
I am a young black man and who knows what he wants
from me: or my dream in which nothing works, not even the lights,
because it's France under the Occupation, and Billie Holiday
sings "I Cried for You" with blue hair on the television
while men in drag fan-dance behind her and young people
grind together in Technicolor on the studio dance floor (when the camera
isn't closing on her pancaked face, her one
gardenia pinned back like blue-rinsed hair), because the Nazis
still allow it and pleasure is such a pretty thing
to watch, and I am hiding in this house with air-conditioning, waiting
for the owners, whom I haven't met, to come home, the lights
to come back on, waking up afraid (just after
they return, turn off a dead black woman's tears)
in the second half of the twentieth century not knowing
the time of day, speaking French to myself, singing.

Lost In a Dream: On Structure and Survival in Reginald Shepherd's "The Lucky One"

Tommye Blount

FOR THERE TO BE A lucky one in Reginald Shepherd's "The Lucky One," survival must be at stake in this time machine of a poem. Here's the deal, a "middle-aged white man" drives up to "a young black man" minding his business. I have questions: what does this man want, who does the young Black man wish himself to be, and why does it all feel so ominous? Shepherd has created a cinematic poem with just eighteen lines to spare, but how? The answer rests within his deft focus on structure, the information held together by a series of time-specific details, by a resonant rhyme system, and by one sentence holding it all together—all of it creating a stanza where shifting time entails the hero's survival . . . or does it?

Yes, Shepherd has his work cut out for him by dedicating much of the poem's eighteen lines to a dream sequence. Of course, I'm thinking of fraught undertakings in lesser poems, in which dreaming gives permission to dole out stream-of-conscious drivel with no way to learn something of the speaker's dilemma. Instead, "The Lucky One" is made of scenes containing historical, pop cultural, and technological referents, thus guiding without laborious exposition. In the opening four lines, for instance, when "[t]he middle-aged white man in a beat-up blue Pinto" *shouts*, "Hey man, what's up?" not only is the beat-up blue Pinto marking a period not too long after the vehicle was discontinued, it still runs well enough to aggressively pull *onto* the curb, but the greeting too pins time to some present-for-the-poem moment—this was published in or shortly before 1994.

"France under the Occupation," Billie Holiday singing live in Technicolor on television—all bits of data that allow the reader to sniff out connections. Tethering the dream in this way, utilizing the narrative shorthand of time-specific details, Shepherd frees up the speaker, allowing this independent variable to be flung from scene to scene when dire circumstances call for it. Now my questions become: is the speaker still who he believes himself to be and will his identity survive the impending doom of "the Occupation?" Before these questions can be answered, or the worst happens, the traveler finds himself hiding in a "house with air-conditioning, waiting / for the owners, whom [he hasn't] met." This air-conditioned house, a technological referent, points toward a more current moment. How did the speaker arrive here? And why is he hiding? At this point in the poem, whether I get an answer isn't as important as this overwhelming dread those questions proffer.

What is clear: he is under siege; needs the rescue only time shifting can offer. Because the two men's races are mentioned at the poem's outset, to hear of *this* young Black man hiding in a stranger's house is troubling. Will his unbeknownst-to-him presence betray him as a threat? Once more, before the scene can play out in the last three lines, another time leap happens, because Billie Holiday is now the dead Black woman on television who gets turned off. Furthermore, the speaker wakes up afraid "in the second half of the twentieth century," yet does waking mean the speaker is done with the dream?

It's certainly clear, Shepherd has resisted the pitfalls of dream drivel by insisting on a referential catalog. Inherent in that volley of historical, pop cultural, and technological happenings, is narrative shorthand. We, the readers, can sense the threat and better ascertain the time period, while the poem maintains its frenetic pacing. Each detail, as in cinema, does a lot of work simply by being present in a scene. Moreover, keeping movies in mind, sound too becomes vital to this poem's cohesive structure.

Rather rhymes, not simply sound, buttress the poem. Take the first and last two lines, each set cinched together by end rhymes: "Pinto" with "up onto" in the first; the gerunds tethering "knowing" to "singing" in the last. Within the rhymes' struggle toward resonance, there is an attempt toward order. Moments at which, deceptively, the poem is temporally stable. Then, inside the dreamscape, slanted rhymes continue a loose structure with words like "Occupation" and "television," "together" and "Technicolor," "pancaked face" and "pinned back." Each word a wobbly bridge toward another. Yet, what's most surprising to me about this dreamscape is the slippage from an aural rhyme to a visual one. Honing in on the resonance from the *blue* Pinto in the beginning, when Billie Holiday appears, she's first described "with blue hair." A little farther down, she's said to have "one gardenia pinned back like blue-rinsed hair." Her blue hair is at first description, then gets promoted to a simile's vehicle four lines down in "like blue-rinsed hair." Similarly, the camera has too promoted its sight: zooming in on the singer, a higher definition. Through this repetition of "blue," are we to make a connection between one troubled vessel (the beat up blue Pinto) and another?

Just as the speaker is on a Sisyphean somnambulist's journey, the sentence too makes its own wayward trip. It begins simple enough, a declarative that establishes the initial interaction. It should end with "me," yet something else happens. Not "then," one of the markers of narrative structure (this happened, then this happened), but ": or" appears, derailing yet widening the sentence's aperture, creating room where there shouldn't be room to meander—say in a dream. Now, Shepherd has purchased real estate and time for all those dependent clauses to flicker scene after scene.

At the center, the tenth line, the alchemy between line and sentence is at its most intense with "isn't closing on her pancaked face, her one." Not only does this line position the syntax so that "her one"—perhaps inference of Holiday as one of the lucky ones, or a depiction of the chanteuse as heroine in wartime, or a fore-shadow of the drug that claimed her life—is sandwiched between the comma and the line's end. Out of this tension between line and syntax, like a film negative, an after image emerges, one presaging the dead Black woman whose tears are turned off later. In "isn't closing on her pancaked face," there is the camera *and* the coffin lid. Her face made up for one viewing before another sort of viewing. A triumphant moment, it *isn't* closing over her, while acknowledging that it will. By the end of the poem, what's at first diva worship becomes death's portent—her death being another time referent for the speaker's trek.

Although he wakes up in the "second half of the twentieth century," the "young black man['s]" physical state remains unfixed as he's speaking French to himself and singing, "unaware of the time of day." An oblivion of "not knowing." More than summation, the ending is symptomatic of an unsettled mind, an unsettled body. Despite the sentence ending with terminal punctuation, the speaker still resides in the dreamscape set off by the colon's door of no return. Is this altered state the escape from the ominous meeting that began the poem? Is this testimony survival's proof, that luck the title promises?

Nights and Days of Nineteen-Something

For Marilyn Hacker

Midsummer with other men's lovers, fumbles
on a living room couch, significance asleep
upstairs: I come through the door, I come
through the door, I came and was

conquered by tensed thighs, taut buttocks.
Asses, asses, lust from lust, a must
of sweat on matted hair, a spill of semen
down my thigh. (Classicism revised, or

what shall we do with a drunken
torso, machine shop of body parts, some
of them functional. Pink petals
of an asshole opening under tongue,

pink cockhead swollen to bursting
purple balloon. It caught in the trees.)
Who am I to think that
I'm not always on my knees

taking in some stranger strayed too far
from what he wouldn't want
to work for, paying out the line
we've always used. *Hey, do you want*

a ride? I'm walking through a field
of safety glass without my shoes; it itches,
like a sneeze. (Say it, no things but in
ideas: desire, denial; define, defiler. Decide,

then choose for me. Mother may I
go down on this man?) The tuck
in my jeans itches afterward, salt
smudge under my knees. This

is for your body made out of words,
the worse for wear if you were there, or
where I wanted me to be. *And where
were you last night, young man?* (Here's

a rumor someone passed along: I believed in
his present tense, wrapped in tinfoil and a tissue
paper ribbon, his cock worn to the right
and the several layers that kept me from it,

the shirt and several layers most of all.)
*If you have many desires your life
will be interesting*, a modernism of poverty
and stained sheets, twin bed he went to

with me, came up for air and other things.
It was never sex I wanted, the grand etcetera
with a paper towel to wipe it up. I wanted him
to talk to me about Rimbaud while

I sucked him off in the park, drunk
as any wooden boat and tasting of old cigarettes
and Bailey's Irish Cream, my juvenilia. *Don't talk
with your mouth full.* (In the clearing

at the bottom of the artificial hill, his two hands
covered every part of me until I couldn't be seen,
a darkness past the burnt-out lamppost.
We came up empty-handed. *You're so empty*

-headed sometimes.) I never wanted love
from him, his needs adhesive, clinging like
old sweat, cold sperm; I never wanted him
to ask anything of me but suck *my big*

white cock. I come home sticky with
his secrecies, wash them all
off. You were my justice, just my means
to sex itself, end justified by the mean

size of the American penis. Just keep going
that way. You'd like to sleep, you'd like to be
left alone for miles of near-misses, missteps, mirrors
in a public bathroom, all mistake

and brief apology. (My lakefront myths of you
all insufficient to the taste of come
lapping my tongue.) The jogging path
curves up into that dark place in the trees

just past the rusted totem pole. Let me
lick salt from white skin in the moon's first light
when it lies brightest: argent, ardent, concrete
and utter falsehood. Comely, my comeuppance,

comfort me: come to mind at any time,
come again for me. Take me to the boy.

On Reginald Shepherd's "Nights and Days of Nineteen-Something"

Charles Stephens

I WANTED TO WRITE ABOUT Reginald Shepherd, because I wanted to carve out a space in his work for myself. We share some aspects of identity: Black and gay; part of his childhood was spent in Georgia, where I've always lived. But I approach Shepherd with some ambivalence. My exploration of some parts of his work for example, may be perceived by his critics and my own, as an affirmation of his views, especially around whiteness and beauty, or even a defense of them. To this I can only respond in two ways: Can one admire the pursuit of beauty, and differ only in what's considered to be beautiful? I don't believe the role of the critic is to provide a psychological diagnosis of the writer, but to arrive at some truth about oneself. And the second point of my defense: if Joseph Beam, who wrote "Black men loving Black men is the Revolutionary Act of the eighties," could publish Shepherd in his 1986 work *In the Life: A Black Gay Anthology*, then who am I to exclude Shepherd from my literary tribe? Though our worldviews may differ, and we may have very different notions of what's beautiful, we do share a commitment to interrogating desire and truth, as shaped by race and pleasure, and that's my point of engagement for his work.

Reginald Shepherd's "Nights and Days of Nineteen-Something" is a poem in part about desire, but more specifically about the truth of desire. And this is what fascinates me most about his work. In the poem, a narrator reflects on a lover, and his own interior process of desiring:

> conquered by tensed thighs, taut buttocks.
> Asses, asses, lust from lust, a must
> of sweat on matted hair, a spill of semen
> down my thigh . . .

Shepherd introduces us into this erotic realm that he conjures through the narrator of the poem. Initially controlled by his desires, as the poem moves, so does the agency of the language:

> It was never sex I wanted, the grand etcetera
> With a paper towel to wipe it up. I wanted him

To talk to me about Rimbaud while
I sucked him off in the park drunk

By decoding desire, stripping it down to its core, Shepherd explores how desire works, and how it hides. Desire, no matter how consuming, is never outside of power, even if it resides within the white phallus. Rimbaud is also key, along with his descriptions of the "big white cock" and the "American penis," bringing together a primal sexuality, the Western canon, and desire into the text. In the poem, the speaker's desire for Rimbaud and his desire for the white phallus are one in the same, a desire for validation, and ultimately transcendence. He leaps from seeking the permission of the mother ("Mother may I go down on this man?") to the fantasy of being commanded by the white father ("I never wanted him to ask anything of me but suck my big white cock"). The frequent reference to fellatio also suggests a relationship to power, not in the sex act itself, but in the erotic charge of surrender, and the satisfying personal agency of shifting and playing with power. This is not to suggest that eroticizing whiteness is inherently subversive; rather in the poem, the awareness of the operations of power may help us find its defects.

Our literary projects may be different; Shepherd once wrote: "I have been oppressed by many things in my life, but not by literature." I at times admire his relentless and unflinching pursuit of beauty. My own pursuit of justice, if not mercy, makes me too vulnerable to the weight of history and the seduction of politics to approach literature detached from my identity. I am then forced to approach Shepherd's work not as a critic, but as a witness, or better yet a moralist, not to judge, but to clarify.

You, Therefore

For Robert Philen

You are like me, you will die too, but not today:
you, incommensurate, therefore the hours shine:
if I say to you "To you I say," you have not been
set to music, or broadcast live on the ghost
radio, may never be an oil painting or
Old Master's charcoal sketch: you are
a concordance of person, number, voice,
and place, strawberries spread through your name
as if it were budding shrubs, how you remind me
of some spring, the waters as cool and clear
(late rain clings to your leaves, shaken by light wind),
which is where you occur in grassy moonlight:
and you are a lily, an aster, white trillium
or viburnum, by all rights mine, white star
in the meadow sky, the snow still arriving
from its earthwards journeys, here where there is
no snow (I dreamed the snow was you,
when there was snow), you are my right,
have come to be my night (your body takes on
the dimensions of sleep, the shape of sleep
becomes you): and you fall from the sky
with several flowers, words spill from your mouth
in waves, your lips taste like the sea, salt-sweet (trees
and seas have flown away, I call it
loving you): home is nowhere, therefore you,
a kind of dwell and welcome, song after all,
and free of any eden we can name

On Reginald Shepherd's "You, Therefore"

Paisley Rekdal

SYNTAX IS THE HEART OF style. We cast a spell through delay or repetition, through inverted phrases, through hypotaxic hierarchy and subordination or parataxic equivalence, through the careful use of punctuation or the total absence of it, through direct statement and extended comparison. Usually a poem is marked by one or more of these strategies, but Reginald Shepherd's "You, Therefore" contains almost all of them. Shepherd's poem is a single sentence that constantly interrupts itself, revising and also embroidering upon its thinking. At times, it eddies around rhymes. At times, it culminates in a pile-up of parenthetical phrases. It even contains two moments of antimetabole or near-antimetabole, in which a phrase is repeated in reversed order, as you can see in the lines : "if I say to you 'To you I say,'" and also "(your body takes on / the dimensions of sleep, the shape of sleep / becomes you)," which create moments of pause in this poem that otherwise speeds through its ever-changing images.

But the question with style is, as always, what purpose it serves the poem's overall meaning. Merely trying on a style is not the same thing as maximizing its surprise, nor is it the same thing as elevating style itself to the level of content. "You, Therefore" is a love poem but also a tricky (future) double elegy for the anticipated loss of the speaker's beloved and also for the fact all forms of love, and all bodies, die. We are stuck in bodies and, as mortal beings, our love must expire as our bodies do. Notice how many references there are to death, to night, to sleep, to the "eathwards journeys" undertaken by snow, even the future and putative disappearance of trees and sea. The human beloved even ceases to be human at all as the poem progresses: "strawberries spread through [his] name," as slowly the beloved changes from a body that "remind[s]" the speaker of spring to a plant itself, to which "late rain clings to [his] leaves," the beloved's self morphing entirely into "a lily, an aster, white trillium / or viburnum . . . white star / in the meadow sky" and finally snow.

Eros, ecosystem, and loss twine together in ways that recall the pastoral elegiac tropes found in the "carpe diem" odes written since Horace's time. Here, the beauty of the natural world is fundamentally attached to its temporality, whether seasonal or diurnal, which may be one reason Shepherd's syntax feels at once so baroque and fast-paced. Each image is gorgeous, at times verging on the overwrought, but each is quickly replaced by a different, equally beautiful vision. We cannot stay with a single natural object or moment of time before Shepherd leaps to another, rushing on to the speaker's next thought as both an act of celebration and avoidance. In that, "You, Therefore" toggles between elegy and ode, its elaborate syntax trying to forestall the end the speaker recognizes as inevitable from the poem's start: "You are like me, you will die too, but not today," Shepherd announces, and every clause and parenthetical that follows becomes an attempt to ward off this mortality, to keep the beloved alive. This may be, I suspect, why the poem ends without a period, trailing off instead into white space. The images may be beautiful throughout, but the poem's lyric tension is created and sustained by the poem's syntax, which in its variability and backtracking for me corresponds with the ephemeral cyclicality of nature itself, and stands in stark relief to the memorial work of human-made art such as painting or music which attempts to immortalize a person through static representation. "You have not been / set to music . . . may never be an oil painting or / Old Master's charcoal sketch," Shepherd writes, and yet, of course, the beloved *has* been memorialized by Shepherd's words, in this poem that reflects both the transitory fact of nature, and the enduring power of desire itself.

MATTHEW LAWRENCE GARCIA

Romero vs. Tapia, 97

WHEN I WAS FIFTEEN, MY best friend C and I got seriously into boxing. That summer there was a buzz around the scene in Albuquerque that felt different from the usual jive of boys wanting to get rich and drive lush lowriders and SUVs, or the old men standing around the bodega chatting up this and that boxeador. It was a shift in the atmosphere that had at its source the fact that our forgotten, nowhere town had not one but two nationally ranked title contenders, Danny Romero and Johnny Tapia, guys with bad blood between them who boxed in the same weight class. Word was they were finally going to fight that July.

My father worked at a local grocery, and one afternoon, while C and I were bumming around the video rental section, Johnny Tapia himself came walking in. He was a real devil from the South Valley who'd disappeared for a while after getting banned for cocaine use, which was normal enough in our city, but he'd been boxing again for a couple of years and building a big reputation. Suffice it to say, when he walked past us, we were completely flashed.

Of course, we'd seen pictures of him in magazines, but I'd never seen someone famous in real life. He wore joggers and a gray tank top and had a Virgin Mary tattoo on his chest with Mary's hands and the crown of her head poking up at his neck. He was smaller than I had imagined, with a smooth cropped head and open brown eyes, but he seemed powerful, wild. C pinched me as Tapia disappeared around a corner, only to return a minute later holding six thick steaks to his chest, pausing to scan the shelves at the end of our aisle.

My father was walking toward us in his red apron, his dark hair combed back. "That vato destroyed a whole display a few weeks back, completely drunk." He stood there akimbo. "If he can't behave, I'm calling security." He was being too loud, baiting Tapia, and I was afraid the boxer would come drop him. My dad was strong, with cut-ass arms from all those morning push-ups, but he stood no chance.

"He isn't doing anything," I said.

"Go home," my father said. He rubbed a hand across his mustache and chin. "There's nothing to see here."

I never talked back to my father, but I couldn't help myself. "You don't know what you're talking about."

My father grabbed my upper arm. "You do not speak to me that way, carajo."

Tapia must have overheard us as he came down the aisle carrying his steaks and a gallon of vodka, his chest puffed and chin jutted, full of menace. My father stared at him hard. But when Tapia got close, he merely grinned, patted my father on the shoulder, and winked.

"Evening mass," he said, moving toward the checkout line. "Gotta go."

My father looked after him, scoffing with contempt, but C and I were spellbound. Most people around town would be rooting for pretty-boy Romero in the upcoming fight, especially the girls, but in that moment, I knew I would be a Tapia fan.

THIS HAPPENED AT the cusp of summer, and my life at the time was pretty grim. See, my father and C's pops were longtime chums from the barrio. That winter, they'd started up with the Army Reserves for a bit of extra cash, and all that training had turned my father into even more of a drill sergeant. From me he demanded discipline, order, and self-improvement. He'd been a hardass even before my mother left us, but now he seemed hell-bent on destroying my social life: no arcade games at the indoor mercado, no hanging out at the community pool watching the girls show off their bikinis. Whereas C's dad mostly just let him be, my father had taken to waking me up that summer at 6 a.m., standing in my doorway and tapping the lip of his coffee mug.

"You can get up and study, or help around the house," he said. "But you're not going to sleep all day, chico. Life is hard, and the sooner you learn that, the better."

C and I had joined the local boxing club earlier that year, wanting to get stronger and wear the cool gear. My father and I argued over this—he preferred I do model UN or even baseball—but eventually he'd given in, and that spring C and I spent two afternoons a week in a swampy gym with Coach Ruiz. Now that it was summer and I couldn't go to the arcade or the pool, C and I started to do more boxing. C had gotten his dad to pony up for two pairs of golden-colored gloves, and we'd take them over to the cottonwood at the back edge of the apartment property and do some pretty legit sparring. Our sessions got intense, pounding on each other's pubescent bodies, drinking in the smell of wet leather from the gloves. When we finished, we'd sit around in the shade and chat about the upcoming fight, which had finally been scheduled for July 17 at the UNLV stadium, after some bullshit with the LV Hilton not wanting to host the event for fear of Mexican and Hispanic fans starting riots. Mostly, though, we talked about Tapia: the rumor that his mother was abducted by a man, raped, and left for dead on the side of the road when he was eight; the early drug use; the fights, of which he'd won 150 as an amateur; and of course his nickname, Mi Vida Loca.

"You can't top that handle," C said, sitting on the front steps with his duffle.

"That's for sure."

By the night of the fight, we'd spent hours sparring and sitting up in my room, looking at boxing magazines, predicting what plan Tapia would have for dealing with Romero's consistent and wearing jabs. It was like the comet that had hovered over us all summer was finally connecting with the earth. C's dad sprang for pay-per-view, a whopping thirty-nine dollars, and was hosting a little party with C's uncles and guys from the shoe factory where C's dad worked.

Early that afternoon, my father brought me a sandwich to my room and said he could wrap a second one for later, if I wanted, to have a snack before I went to C's. He touched the back of my head, and I felt a quick tenderness for him. His shift started at 1 p.m., but he was planning to stop by C's after work. He didn't care about the fight but was always glad to have a rum on ice and relax in friendly company. I said no thanks to the second sandwich because there would be all kinds of *amazing* food at the party. His expression hardened.

"Just know if the fight is not over by 10:30, you still have to go to bed."

After he left the room, my face turned hot. I knew that if I complained about the curfew, he might not let me see the fight at all. I grabbed a sheet of paper from my desk and calculated when the fight would end if it went all twelve rounds. It seemed like I wouldn't miss anything. I breathed out slowly and leaned back in the chair.

Around four, I bounced up the two flights to C's place and found his mother tacking colorful streamers on the wall. There was a red cooler with beers on the squat coffee table; a big plate of the microwave taquitos they always ate, smelling like grease and corn; a massive fruit salad; a pot of posole; and a platter of tamales with a covered bowl of red chili steaming next to it. C's dad sat watching the first undercard in a checked shirt, sleeves rolled, and a Tecate in hand. He nodded to us.

"Manny, C, órale run over to the bodega and pick up whatever other snacks you want. And get me a pack of cigarettes." He was in high spirits. He pulled out two twenties, which was unheard of, in C's house or especially mine. My father didn't earn much and constantly worried about money. That was probably part of why he was so stiff and serious, having to raise a son alone with no safety net, though at the time, I simply wished he was more like C's dad.

C snatched the bills and we raced out of the apartment.

At the bodega, C grabbed Twizzlers, popcorn, tortilla chips, and BBQ chips. "And do we go Fanta or Jarritos? I want to say Fanta, but somehow Jarritos seems more appropriate. I can't imagine Tapia drinking a Fanta."

"Me neither," I said.

We put our wares on the counter, and C asked for the Marlboros. We were obviously underage, but the bodega owner sold to us because she knew C's dad would kick his ass if he caught C smoking. Like the rest of the neighborhood, the bodega was governed by the laws of parental authority mixed with a swirl of

Latin-American-Catholic mysticism and Our-Lady-of-Guadalupe worship. The owner lowered her radio and asked us who was going to win the fight. She'd probably heard that C's dad had ordered it on pay-per-view.

We assured her that it would be Tapia, the dark horse, obviously. She laughed and informed us that Romero was in better training and the more polished of the two.

Outside, our bag of snacks swinging from my hand, I told C she just said that because her granny ass thought Romero was handsome.

"Not like he'd bang her with a twelve-foot pole," C said.

"You don't say it like that," I told him. "'Touch her with.'"

"Whatever, man. I'm hallucinating. I want this thing to start or I'll punch myself in the face. Hand me one of those Jarritos." There was a bottle opener on the bodega's brick wall. He popped the top and took a long drink. "I bet he does get a lot of pussy, though."

The sun was heavy and beating down. We passed the old shoe factory and went under the overpass toward the apartment house. C was chattering away as usual, but I was hardly paying attention, imagining myself sitting right next to the fan with my cold Jarritos and watching Tapia come into the ring, throw some crisp air punches, wiggle his head from shoulder to shoulder. We practically ran up the steps to the fourth floor.

"Órale," C's dad said. "Good timing. Last undercard just finished."

A few guys sat around holding paper plates with taquitos and dollops of salsa, half-eaten tamales, their pearling Tecates marshaled atop the coffee table. My father was in the kitchen with one of C's uncles, laughing at something, a glass in front of him. He shot me a wink. He still had on his white, short-sleeved button-up from work, his hair combed back smoothly. He looked tired, but I was glad to see him in a good mood.

The crowd on TV was buzzing in the lull before the main event. C and I stuffed Doritos and Twizzlers down our throats, chased with slugs of Jarritos. Finally, Romero sauntered down the ramp in his gold and red-lined robe, the hood low over his eyes. Tapia came next, and the crowd erupted as the two fighters eyed each other, getting up in each other's faces with all that trash talk. We leaned forward and grabbed our knees. A fat dude in a plastic chair next to the TV started punching his palm, saying, "Come on." C gave me a light smack on the shoulder as the ref talked to the fighters, and then the bell rang.

The fighters came right at each other like they were both set on swift, explosive destruction, or believed that was possible. The word that came to mind was "unleashed," though it was more than that. They were magnetized toward each other in the center of the ring. Romero launching a heavy cross. Then Tapia coming right back with his own, deflecting off Romero's shoulder. But after an initial flourish of blows, they drew back and became more calculating, trying to read each other. Tapia threw measured, swaggering jabs that flew from his shoulder like birds, his black trunks swishing. Romero slid out and jabbed back, his hair perfectly combed and puffed. He did his pretty-boy routine, bouncing on his toes with more lightness than Tapia, which annoyed me. I kept waiting for Tapia to catch him in one of those shuffles and drop him flat.

The announcer spoke loudly over the roaring fans, saying no heavyweight fight of the moment could draw a crowd as big as this junior bantamweight match, so fierce was the blood between these two men, so high the expectations. I felt a swell of pride. This was an event for our neighborhood and our city, and C and I had a special place in it, because we were boxers ourselves. And because we knew what was what. Tapia was a real fighter, and he'd had to overcome so much, like the loss of his mother. Sure, he was hot-dogging a bit, but only when moving away. He was all form when he got close, working tight spaces with the concentration of someone putting together a model car. It was especially beautiful because he wasn't as strong as Romero, lacked his musculature, that extra power Romero housed in his round shoulders.

Early on, Tapia leaned down from his corner to one of the reporters and said, "He doesn't hit that hard," and we just about lost it. One of the guys from the shoe factory was telling C's dad that Romero was hitting hard as fuck and that Tapia was a clown. Apparently only C and his dad and I were for Tapia. I cursed the other men in my head, pinche know-nothings, and tried to hold down the nervy mess of chips and sugar in my stomach. At some point, my father had joined C's mom on the couch. She didn't care about the fight either, and they were holding glasses of rum and talking, oblivious to the frenzy on TV.

At the height of the fight, it wasn't clear who would win. Romero landed a few mean hooks that Tapia almost seemed to invite, so lax was his protective stance. Even so, two of the commentators were saying that Tapia was fighting the prettier match. Everything was moving so fast. It felt like only a few minutes, though it was suddenly the end of the ninth round. I turned to C and asked him if he was keeping a point count, but he shook his head. I feared Romero might be ahead on landed hits because he relied on so many jabs without taking much risk. One of the announcers had Romero ahead on his card.

I thought it would slow down then; the fighters looked tired. I could feel their limbs getting cold, heavy, knew the sensation from my own amateur experience and afternoons with C. Yet they had their third or fourth wind. And Romero got in a few big crosses. The fighters offered a last flourish in the waning seconds, and for a moment, as Tapia dipped clear of a wild cross, I thought he might sneak in that knock-out blow that would end it without going to the cards. But then we heard the bell. This was it. The camera split and zoomed in on both fighters' bruised and puffy faces. People milling. The announcer boomed in, reading off the cards, then let unfurl, "to the IBF and WBO Junior Bantamweight champion of the world, Johnny Tapia." We exploded. Tapia's eyes welled with tears, his arms flying up. C stood on the couch and started doing a chicken dance, then hopped back down and grabbed my shoulders. We felt good. I mean really good. We and we alone had picked Tapia to be the winner, and he was our champion.

WHEN EVERYTHING CALMED down on TV, the men moved to the kitchen to drink more, but C and I were still in high gear.

"So what now?" he said, though it was pretty obvious to both of us—we needed to relive the fight. My father was in the kitchen laughing with C's dad, and even though it was only 9:50, I asked him if it was okay to go down to the cottonwood for a little sparring.

His eyes narrowed, but then he surprised me. "Yeah, okay. I guess we can stay out till 11:00, ¿qué no?" He checked his watch in that reflective way he had then turned back to C's dad.

We grabbed C's gloves and went downstairs to the cottonwood, which was illuminated by the parking lot lights. The air was still warm and the dark blue of underwater depths, but not too hot. Someone had knocked over one of the trash-cans next to the parking lot, and there were yellow burger wrappers scattered about, the buzz of distant traffic.

"So look, I know you want to be Tapia," C said, "but I take him on the fact I started us on the boxing."

"Dude, you can't just be Tapia." I swung my gloved fist and got him right above the stomach. I'd meant it as a playful thing, but it was a hard shot, and C sat right down on the ground.

"Shit, man."

"Sorry."

"Say warning."

"I didn't mean it so hard."

"Right in the sternium."

I didn't correct him.

He held a glove up to his mouth and let out a quick cough. Then he pushed himself up. "I think I'd look better covered in tattoos than you."

I had never imagined myself with a tattoo. My father had one, a tiny bird on his wrist, maybe a magpie. I'd asked him about it, but he would close up, look away. Though, I always thought of birds as somehow connected to us, like a family crest.

Over in the parking lot next to a purple lowrider with chrome rims, a couple of guys were watching us from the shadows. They moved toward us now, vaulting the small fence that separated the apartment houses. Both had shaved heads, white tank tops, and the big, ballooned khaki Dickies that hoods wore.

"'Sup, carnales," the shorter one said.

I'd seen him around, though I didn't know his name. The lowrider was his. "Hey," I said.

"You fucking cheap-shotted your boy." He held out his hands. "Truchas, no?"

"Sorry," I said, looking back at C. In the distance, I could hear everyone in C's apartment talking loudly over the radio. The taller guy coughed and spat.

"Bueno," the short one said. He had a cigarette in his mouth. "Pues show us something." He threw a few air punches. He was thick-bodied, more chubby than ripped, but he seemed strong.

C looked at me, then back at them. "Okay." He tapped my gloves with his, and we squared off. C moved with his shoulders too tight, lacking his usual good form. I felt tense too. C started working me with his jab and then tried to land a right hook to my shoulder, but I slid out and gave him a rabbit punch on the side of the neck. He moved out of that and then put two jabs straight to my raised hands.

"Ha, these diaper rashes are cute," the short one said. "Mira." He held his hand out to C for his gloves.

C took them off and handed them over, not really looking at the guy.

"I was Golden Gloves, carnales, I'll go easy. Just show you some juice." He let his cigarette dangle like he was in a movie. "Like your gloves, gueyes, ha." He cinched the second glove with his teeth, somehow not dropping his cigarette. His eyes had purple rings like he hadn't slept. As he came toward me, I started to move a bit, throwing a few light body jabs. He was obviously stronger than me, and at least ten years older, but I felt pretty good about my skills. At the gym, I had a reputation as a quick learner and was already getting better than C. If nothing else, I was a lot faster than this guy.

He shook his shoulders as he got closer, head bobbing. I let him land a few on my blocking hands, and he clipped me on the side of the head, but then I ducked back in and landed a few body shots, and he backpedaled, surprised.

"You're quick, eh?" He turned to his friend and laughed. "Pon las luces, guey, let's make this fun, like that fight on TV, no? Light us up."

The tall guy hopped back over the fence, holding up his Dickies at the back, and went to the lowrider. He shined the ghostly headlights on us.

C leaned over to me. "Be Tapia," he whispered. "For now."

Silly as it was, that did feel good. But my thoughts jumped from Tapia in the ring to the man in the grocery store, who'd felt no need to flex or push things. And the last thing I wanted was to escalate the situation. The short guy threw his cigarette on the ground, then came hopping up, shuffling his feet. There was far too much seriousness in his eyes, even though his lips were smiling.

Back in those days, I tried to keep a low profile, always cautious of certain types of people. There was a reason parts of Albuquerque were called "The War Zone" and "Red Barelas." Now, as an adult living hundreds of miles away, that part of my life seems less than real, in that I don't come into contact with the kind of guys who will want to box the shit out of a little kid to feel like the man. But essentially that's what he did.

At first, I squared him away with jabs and kept him from getting any shots in, but then he cocked back and launched the hardest punch he could, a pachuco haymaker. It bounced off my arms, well blocked, but it rattled me. I flashed to Tapia cocking his big hook and unloading a haymaker like that on Romero's raised gloves. Flashed to the simple bulk of Romero's shoulders. But also to mess, chaos, like how they came at each other at the beginning of the fight. My stomach was heavy, and my arms were shaking. I took a steadying breath.

"Too much, eh?" He had the slight makings of a mustache over his lip. He came in again and threw another haymaker, and instinct prevailed as I dropped a straight jab to his chin. I didn't put that much on it, but it was enough to rile the guy.

"Mocoso, ya no entiendes nada, no?" He put his mouth to his right glove and opened the wrist, then slid it under his arm to pull it off. With the glove still in his armpit, he reached behind his back into his waistband and pulled out a small, silver revolver. He didn't point it at me, but my heart stopped as he set it onto the ground and got into his fighting position again.

"Now," he said.

I tried to pull myself together, but I couldn't. I had gone soft with the fear. He unloaded three or four crisp face shots. I'm not exactly sure how many because I was soon on the ground, not knocked out, but out of it nonetheless. I felt like I'd had my eyes closed the whole time, though I hadn't. I put a glove to my mouth and there was blood. As I tried to rise, the gravel rubbed against my knees. So this was how it felt to be punch drunk. I looked over and C was taking small steps backward. My right eye socket started to blare a red-hot sun, like someone was jamming a fire poker into it.

The tall guy came up with a spliff and put a hand to the boxeador's shoulder. "Ya guey, he's a little kid."

The short guy took off the gloves. He called C over and handed them to him. Took a big breath of air and then touched his little mustache. "That's how you give it to that mocoso next time he gives you a cheap shot." He patted C on the head, went over to his gun by the tree, and slid it back into his waistband.

The tall one puffed his paper worm. It's sweet pot smell reached me in a sudden wave. "Good evening, fellas," he said, and followed his friend over the fence to the lowrider. As they were leaving, C helped me up, then helped me take off the gloves. His hands were shaky.

"That guy was a G, man," he said. "It's good you went down."

WHEN WE RETURNED to the apartment, the guests were gone, and it was quiet. C's dad was sitting on the couch watching the late news with the sound turned low. When he saw us, his face dropped.

"Why you beat up Manny, boy?" He came to me and touched my face with his soft, large hands.

"I didn't," C said.

"Where's my dad?" I asked.

C's mother came down the hall and looked at me. "Oh."

"It was some guys," C said. "They had a gun. They wanted to box us."

"What guys?" C's dad said. "Are they still here?"

"Just some thugs from around. I think they're gone."

"Did my dad leave?" I said.

"He went to the corner for a bottle of rum," C's mother said.

C's parents exchanged a look, and then C's mother turned off the TV as his dad went to the window and gazed down at the parking lot. I'm sure he wanted to rush out and make a show of wanting to confront the thugs, but he was a smart man and knew he couldn't do anything, not with guys like that. My father, on the other hand, would already have been out the door, his footsteps echoing in the stairwell. That day at the grocery with Tapia, he'd barely been able to control himself; certainly he wouldn't have backed down from a couple of neighborhood thugs, pistol or not. I knew this in my soul, and it frightened me. What had happened outside wasn't sport, but only violence, pain, and I felt disgusted thinking about more.

C's mother went to the kitchen and came back with an icepack. She was fussing over me, and I thought I would cry. My eye was throbbing, my stomach swirling. And then, out in the hall, someone was whistling, the lilting tune of one of my father's favorite boleros. When the door opened, he looked at me for a moment, his eyes widening, his mouth hardening.

"Carajo, what happened?"

Then, before anyone could say anything, I stepped forward, feeling my hands tingle, and said, "C's getting good. It was my fault. I need to learn better blocking skills." I didn't look at anybody, feeling the words hang there.

Behind me, C's father sniffed loudly, and I turned. He righted his bulk in his chair, put his hands on his thighs. "Ay, these chamacos need to be more careful. You know how they are."

My father looked to me almost like trying to confirm the statements or assess the damage, and I was grateful to have the icepack to hide behind as I nodded. I caught C's father's eye but looked away immediately. I felt a rush of embarrassment for my father, so easily swallowing this lie in front of C and his family. But mostly I was humiliated because the lie was so necessary to protect my father. And seeing that C's dad thought the same hurt even more. The shame burnt in my cheeks, and I was afraid my father would see; I moved the ice pack more toward my nose. The pain still strobed in my eye socket. I couldn't imagine ever wanting to be hit again, not in play nor actuality. The ice pack slipped from my hand to my lap, and I quickly picked it up and reapplied it.

My father put the rum bottle on the coffee table then and bent down to my face, took my chin in his hand.

"I'm fine," I said, jerking away. "It's nothing."

For a second my father looked taken aback, and I thought he would reprimand me for snapping at him, but he stayed calm, taking my chin again and angling my face, gently testing my cheek with his thumb, a gesture that brought to mind my mother licking a finger, wiping a smudge from my face. Years later, after my father's passing to cancer this past March, I would think of this night upon seeing a magpie on my balcony railing, and I would feel an overwhelming sense of sadness at the distance that first began opening between us there in C's apartment. A distance that came from this lie, but also from the clarity of how I was different from my father, from the thug outside, even from this neighborhood.

He let go of my chin. "Let's go home, yeah?" His face so close to mine I could smell his breath, feel his heat.

Translation Folio

JAN WAGNER

Translator's Introduction

David Keplinger

In 2017 Berlin-based poet Jan Wagner and I completed our eight-years-in-the-making *The Art of Topiary*, selecting his poetry since the beginning of his career, work we'd done wholly over email. By the time Jan and I finally met in Germany that summer, the book was at the printer and we had never met in person or even spoken on the phone. I don't know why that was the case—at a time when even Skype may have made our task easier.

That very distance, however, seemed to fuel the work with each packet I'd receive from him, his lines scanned for me and translated literally, offering me (as he insisted) the freedom to shift the syntax and diction to fulfill the demands of his rhymes, his intricately engineered responses to traditional forms. Sestina, sonnet, haiku, sapphic ode, prose poem, rhymed quatrain, and free verse were invited to the party. In the fall of 2017, just after our meeting and on the eve of the publication of *The Art of Topiary*, Wagner was awarded one of Germany's most prestigious honors, the Georg Büchner Prize, conferred upon a major writer whose contributions to German Literature align with the importance of Paul Celan, Günther Eich, Günther Grass, Ingeborg Bachmann, Max Frisch, and others who have received the award. The prize honors "writers in the German language who have notably emerged through their oeuvre as essential contributors to the shaping of contemporary German cultural life." It catapulted Wagner to the highest status among his peers.

In the United States, Wagner's poetry has grown to enjoy a remarkable appreciation. With that in mind, we set out to complete a new selection of his work from several new books published since 2017. This has culminated in *Wisp*, whose very title suggests a special attention to the ephemeral, the impermanent, encased in the curio cabinets of fixed forms. Over the period of about a year, between the summers of 2022 and 2023, Wagner and I set out on our usual course, working over email and exchanging notes in written form. When we had had a rough draft of the manuscript, we met in Berlin in the summer of 2023 and read together at a public event. The poems published here in *Copper Nickel* were among our offerings.

During the week we spent together, Jan and his wife, Maritta, drove me out to the village where they have—among other writers and escapees of Berlin—restored an old cottage, somewhere near the Madlitz location of his poem published here. During a walk through the wooded areas surrounding the village, the three of us looked down and realized that the path we were tromping over was literally covered with tiny frogs, just born things, hopping madly in every direction to grab their first bearings in the world or hurl themselves out of our way. Horrified that we were now the giants come to crush them heartlessly in this fairy tale, we all instantly froze where we stood, and then it was just the little frogs, and the twilight falling, and the nearby woods, and the wind. And us: three colossi with their hands out, standing quietly on top of a just-born, tender, terrified, discombobulated world.

So it is in the poetry of Jan Wagner, committed in his work over twenty-five years to capturing the moment of surprise, the comic or tragic falling away of appearances, as in the title poem, "Wisp," where the gym teacher's comb-over blows wrongways in the wind, leaving him in "a white panic, / a kite, torn away on its string." All throughout these poems, we find these creatures, themselves not wholly innocent of violence, exposed to a cool, human brutality, the mole-slayer and the cudgeling villager, the bruising roughhousing of the young.

Wagner and I write very differently; often I'm entranced by his diction and the sheer acrobatics of his writing, something out of Hopkins or Heaney. The work is a kaleidoscope of sound. Always it serves as a way of distracting the reader *away* from the decorum and formality that poetry often imposes—suspending our conditioned beliefs about ourselves and our nature so that a deeper intimacy is possible—and we enter into worlds that are, more and more in this later work, revealing the pre-language chthonic realms, some thrumming undertow beneath the waves of culture and progress. The nakedness of the teacher's bald head. The threatening animal under its tin ceiling. What is brought into the light of day receives the day in surprise and wonder.

marten

you can slip with him inside this musty cave,
the dovecote, he is so slim, as the case

may be, marten, an intruder, robber
amidst martyrs, all the gentle rabble,

the cooing messengers, dove after dove
uncorked and drunk by him, this real life

gargantua, while hens flutter all around,
and flutter, flutter, while all around

they flutter and flutter, with sull-
ied bib, until all is silent and full

to perfection; too fat from blood and world
and news to escape through the whorled

hole, a crack, condemned to lean back
into his own achievement, with no lack

of satisfaction and guiltlessly napping
like a cannibal, until someone lifts the ceiling;

and there, with cudgel and pitchfork,
flail, scythe, spade, axe and pitch-torch,

there they are, with shotgun and pedigreed dog:
the audience, beside themselves, agog.

wisp

more often now they lean forward
with advice: suggesting onion stock, fresh
cow pat, dog-milk and birch-juice,
crushed flies. but the naked crest
rises like a rock when the sea withdraws.

with dignity to go bald, to shine,
proud like an ostrich egg in the cabinet of wonder!
not like the old men on the beach
with those dismal final spirals of hair
around the dome of the head—

or the austere mr. s. who taught us
numbers and physical exercises,
but so tiny, that, when he turned his back,
the tallest of us ventured a leapfrog
over him: a gust of wind seized

the one wisp, let it flutter for meters
like telephone-scribblings, closing credits,
and so on and so forth; and his face:
there it flies, a white panic,
a kite, torn away on its string.

crows-ghazal

after the death of the friend he saw crows
everywhere he looked. even before, crows
were always happening, but not like now—
he stepped out of the church; there were crows
on the signs, or blackening breakers, shadows
encircling the bus, a veritable crow
escort straight out of the city, like the tailcoats
of conductors, who conjure for soloist-crows
and crows-choir a musical score, like he composed
with the stolid, hobbling, hopping, crows-
quadrille behind him. or banned at the doors
of the bakery, when enshrouded in crows
he asked for bread; on the park bench, in throes
and gestures, like a widow in sicily, crows
for her sleeves. he forgot the words for *covers*
and *cloud*, for *clotted milk* and *snow*,
and moved as if a blackout down the avenues,
as a whirl, biblical, somber, as if a crows-
tornado, a black top, and slept turned-down-
low like a city in wartime, wakened by crows
even before the day broke open. he'd have to
decide. he would decide with the crow-
ing roosters whether to stand up, and to go,
or like a ruined castle settled under crows
against a hillside, to hunker; as an october
field, to fall and be a resting place for crows.

madlitz elegy

in the morning the mole-slayer haunts
in his yellow coat, destroys the barrows,
and a few high-voltage poles like saints
bless the land. in the jewelry of the eaves,

the wind plays dice or draws lots,
and forestry machines creep through the woods
like protozoic life, slower than moss.
only once around the lake, and you are old.

the cows on the swamp-pastures rust
like washed-up buoys or shipwrecks
and only the woodpecker remains at his post.
you exist because a deer sees you, a fox.

in its woodchip cuttings lies the fallen giant
and the ducks drink darkness in the waves.
in the morning the mole-slayer haunts
in his yellow coat, destroys the barrows.

—translated from the German by David Keplinger

ALLYSON STACK

Fossil Fuel

WHAT HAPPENED TO THE GIRL who went home with the man in a kilt? Who made love to the tall, Scottish stranger—thin curve of his body an open scythe? Then stole away in the ghost light of dawn, suitcase packed with cocktail dresses, an iron skillet, cutlery, a bottle of pills. Aspirin, quaaludes, ecstasy and ephedrine. A confection of chemical commands: stay numb, fall asleep, make love, keep driving.

Some say she returned that afternoon. Circling back along the highway, back to the slow blue bang of you whose fingers filled the hollows of her spine as she rocked against that narrow bed. Hip to thigh, muscle to bone. Each night they say they hear her honeyed hum, soft shudder of her shoulder-blades like wings. She flutters: a bony butterfly beneath the pin of your touch.

Others say she kept going. That she drove until she ran out of road, stopping where hot tar yields to the violent tumble of the sea. Then stood knee-deep in ocean foam and tried to wash away your scent. A musk of yeast and rainwater. But still you lingered, lodged in the sloping clefts and shadows of her body—a secret other—trapped in the dark and tangled tresses of her hair.

Or perhaps she fled to West Texas. Seduced by smooth thrusts of oil drills, she sits by the roadside and watches their gliding slip and climb. Jealous of the earth she demands to know that womb's dark secret: how to replace clear sap with viscous black. How to keep men coming back for more?

Each night they say she lies alone. Wedged beneath a darkness barbed with stars, she waits. Fingertips seeking out the bruises on her thighs, yellowed echo of you, tender ghost . . . she presses them, hard, driving the sweet ache home.

REBECCA ENTEL

What She Was Saying

Swallowing castor oil didn't work, she learns while playing in the sand next to the circle of beach chairs where grandmothers talk. Their legs show maps of their lives she can't yet decipher.

Later she hears married mothers call theirs *D & Cs*. Those who were young and unmarried call theirs *abortions*.

She has always lived in words, but the stories she remembers best, these, are scripted in invisible ink. By a finger in dry sand with the wind approaching: not to be saved. She always remembers the *D* is *dilation*, but somewhere she loses the *C*.

She knows it's different, but when her half-sister's fibroid-ed uterus breaks two lasers before it can all, in pieces, be taken, she realizes she's never heard a man who wasn't a doctor speak the word *hysterectomy*.

Someone once told her Emma Goldman gave the same speeches in English and Yiddish but was arrested for the Yiddish ones, because They didn't know what she was saying. The charge was *lecturing on forbidden medical questions*. Maybe she'll ride the rattling Blue Line far enough west with a stone in her hand to place on the grave, where Goldman's body had been returned twenty years after the woman was deported.

To save can be transitive or intransitive. This is the kind of sentence, she knows, for which people hate (women) English teachers like her. She has always lived in words, wielding language like a wand. It just means a verb that can take or not take an object. She uses *just* a lot to welcome in her most unsure students—like a wand, not a weapon. It just means someone can save something or someone can just save. The object can be oneself.

Once on a plane, going farther than she'd gone before, she watched a man practice Mandarin on the back of his napkin—"Characters, not letters," he told her—and she wondered, still wonders, what it would be like to give or receive a word that could not crack apart.

Maybe she'll travel long enough to reach a place where the rivers haven't dried to bones; the mountains haven't blurred to flames; where the ocean doesn't daily send its wind churning to find its proper name, to swallow then spit out homes; far enough from this place to one, if there were just one, where to save oneself/to save for oneself/saving hasn't become a sentence.

Pointing Fingers

THE BABY BEGINS WALKING, AND she is compelled by all the multi-colored squares on the screen to kiss them with her fingertip, to share pictures and unpunctuated sentences swelling with pride. And a bit of sass to show she was never really worried, not really, as she always said she wasn't. Responses stack and stack, many meant to be supportive but actually quite rude. She wonders if anyone will notice which she hangs a heart on, which just a generic like.

The baby isn't really a baby. It has taken a long time, twice the time others waited, to reach this day of announcement on the multi-colored squares.

Put that thing down, she hears the husband say, and she slides the phone into her back pocket, where it will continue to light up and chime against her butt cheek. But he is talking to the baby, who can now get into the room they never go into with the miniature glass sloth collection he inherited from his grandmother. He steps across the little-used threshold to inspect the baby-handled sloth. They had hoped for something else from the prim and mean grandmother, to help with the house and the baby specialist copays, but they had gotten sloths. Once he determines no damage, he leans low to take the baby's hand, and they mini-step back to where she is, both of their faces taut with concentration and wonder. The phone somersaults out of her pocket, and she realizes she has missed the moment to snap a picture. Still, they all smile at each other before the baby remembers something terrifying, and the house fills with wailing they cannot stop.

·

THE baby navigates the uneven threshold to the screened-in porch, with its splintery floor they've tried to cover with old bath mats. A sudden daredevil, he throws his weight against the screen door and tumbles into the yard the size of a carpet remnant. At least, she tells the husband, the former owner had fenced in a dog from the broken concrete of the driveway. The grass is a carpet, a bed, she lies, knowing it's a teeming world of creatures that hides sharp edges and tiny corpses.

Here's a purple-veined flower she'd never seen in their yard before. Here's a piece of mulch in the shape of Florida. Here's a feather. Here's a broken acorn that leaves a dot of blood on her fingertip. Here are crunchy weed fragments that might be dead worms. Here's a pebble that, on closer inspection, is a baby frog the size of her fingernail. The baby's fists bring all of it into the house.

The husband wiggles his finger between the baby's lips to see what he might be hiding in his cheeks, but she tells him to leave the baby alone. Isn't this what they have waited for?

She chooses memes of cats delivering dead birds at doorsteps and receives a tide of laughing or *o*-mouthed faces.

They cannot find the frog.

•

THE doctor is pleased with the walking news but not enough to stop the upcoming tests. The pre-exams continue, a chunk of an hour in which the smooth baby in nothing but his diaper stretches and twists to be released from her arms while doctors run cold metal disks over his bare skin. Lists and lists of questions.

One set of tests, and then another scheduled at a hospital in a neighboring city, where they'd once gone to see a play about a dictator written by the husband's boss's nephew and driven home in blinding rain. Before the baby.

I don't think there's anything wrong, the husband says. Maybe we should stop with all these tests.

The doctor looks at her, assuming she's the one who spends all the time with the baby and sees things the husband doesn't. Are you sure, he asks. He doesn't know the husband is always telling her to watch more, especially in the yard.

She wants to agree with the husband. She wants to wait for the baby to decide to do the next thing, to finally say *mama* or anything at all, taking his time, like with the walking. But her voice twists into the one that for more than two years, before the walking, told the multi-colored squares her baby was just a lazy man who wanted her to do everything for him—unconcerned, sarcastic. We think he ate a frog, she says.

•

AND so they will wait and see. She hears the husband on his phone. If it weren't the right decision, he says, the doctor wouldn't have let us make it, right? She says nothing to the squares, but some of them hear things and graffiti her profiles with links, each of which is constructed with a hard-to-pronounce name and the word *disorder*. She decides her pockets aren't deep enough and leaves the phone in a drawer.

They will wait and see. The baby a mysterious deity whose motives they can't possibly understand but have to accept. The baby a collection of hiding places.

She arranges the flower and the acorn shards and the mulch and the feather and the crunchy weeds that might be dead worms on one of the bath mats. She was never able to see constellations as a kid but always followed pointing fingers toward the speckled sky.

Each time the screen door thwacks, she turns and waits for the uncurling of a tiny fist.

CHRISTEN NOEL KAUFFMAN

When I Google the Artist's Life

the internet suggests a breakup with mothering
in order to find myself, as if the monster in my rib-

cage is waiting for the right kind of atmosphere,
a moratorium on feces and fruit puffs. if only

that was the thing. if only I could release its spiked tail
in the middle of a grocery store, sit down on the stoop

of some middle school drop-off howling myself
into autonomy. the internet says I've been suppressing

this desire, holds my daughter up by the foot to say
see see see but I reclaim her, show her a system

for polishing her teeth. the truth is somewhere
between god and my neighbor's gun, but the internet

shows statistics on happiness, slips a digital finger
below the curve of my breast, asks me what wild

could live there. imagine when we tell them
about mythology. imagine when the light hits

an iris pod, any crack can scatter its seeds. once,
I painted the opossum because I could, entrails marked

by a passing car, the baby asleep in a sling. I have
been monstrous like my father and his father

splitting wood with a sharpened ax, each cut
a scattering in spite of.   in celebration.

CAROL QUINN

Employment Application for the Position of Dishwasher by Marina Tsvetaeva, 1941

There are dishwashers with history
and dishwashers without history.

A dinner plate is also a tabula rasa.

Better a shot of vodka
than a bullet.

Marina Ivanovna knows
she hasn't quite convinced them.

There is no one on the other side
of words—
                            or rather,

those she thought were there
no longer are. The words

are smooth, flat stones
that skim the surface.

They may spark song
from a sheet of ice but still

fall short of the other shore.

DANA ISOKAWA

Meditation on Distance at the Cocktail Party

All night I watch faces,
watch the sippers sip their wine, the hoverers hover.
When they speak to me, their eyes slide by

as if window shopping:
half interested in what's inside, half interested
in their own reflection.

When I was a child, always so serious, too quiet,
my father used to ask me, What are you thinking?
and my mind would steam up

like spectacles in a hot restaurant.
Zŏushén 走神, the Chinese word for spacing out, means
the spirit walks, and tonight I imagine

my spirit rises from the bench of my body
and drifts out to the courtyard,
past the facts and retorts and shoes,

up the hill, beyond the charmers and wits,
and flows back into the body's bottle
stranger than before.

If I came back as that man pontificating on the lawn,
that woman sermonizing by the stairs, what would I say,
what would I care about?

How does anyone dream feel think reason—
even my sisters, even my brother doubles
if I had them, even you as you stand next to me

and drink your water like I drink mine.
Think of asymptotes: the swoop
                    and then the permanent narrowing—

          the line never meets the axis the chorus the other.
Some days I feel closer to others,
                    like neurons growing toward one another,

          a coral reef of connection—and some days
it's more like those machines that shoot tennis balls at you
                    so you can practice your reply:

          the neon balls sailing over the net again
and again into unanswered space,
                    collecting in the corner, aglow.

CAROLYN OROSZ

Labor

We have done all the picnic activities,

have watched the cars pull in and out
of the parking lot and the little dandelion-headed girl
squat over the fountain waiting for it to turn on, gushing.

I have been scolded for opening my mouth in the river
because: feedlots.

Today the sun is high, yellow, photo-toxic.
The water vapor rises white-hot forever
from the smokestacks at the biomass plant.

Out here—large-scale agriculture,
& California who has turned her lights off.

We are waiting for the revelation—
a place where there is nothing to do,
in which the verses do nothing,

in which the screens sit in a corner
and we kneel all, prayerfully.

Here I am waiting.
As if I have not had my own hand in it.

It was the land of fruit and honey,
we were drowning in that honey.

CINTIA SANTANA

ponding

I will give proof of my zeal: one anthropocene day, I tore off in my car to see the
   blue-green
ice, unable to cure myself. The pond, a property, upstate. I could not bear to lose.
   So that
the ice wheezed when I walked atop it. And something else. The black-black rock,
   the banks,
the high-end plaque. Extracted. Present. Return as if from peril. The roots of a
   vanished oak
rose under the ice. Spidered forth from my feet. I heard the ice stretch, so I
   dropped to listen
more closely. To press my cheek against the surface. To feel it burn. Alas,
   inevitably, I thought
of Professor [ ], a reptile who teaches at Yale. I'd made him admit he has no idea
   where winter
winters. To this place he cannot imagine some part of me takes flight each year
   faster.

ISAAC PICKELL

When your mother loses another apartment

I'd heard their *welcome* together, another word designed
          to be unimpeachable: the same, caught
          in the snare of the smell of change,
          that lingering sharpness that follows

being scrubbed to suit someone else's sense of neutral.
          It was loud, and I was little, and nothing
          about this felt like that concept you are
          always supposed to share, a lazy hailing

permeating tile stained the same yellow they were painted,
          stripped yellow by grease and fingertips,
          nostalgia and old cigarettes, and the yellow
          nostalgia of old cigarettes, filtered sun and

dripping water. Home. Bright things. Bright, yellow things.
          The least I knew I knew from listening
          to the birdsong and bug hum I'd grow
          used to but not enough to hush them over

with the patina of ambiance: yes, we taught you all about
          the orchestra, but these crickets chirp
          & yes, there are crows where mom lives
          now, but don't be afraid of any on-the-nose

metaphor. Like watching someone carve a sculpture
          out of affection, each word tuliped
          within a careful design designed to
          disappear, the wisps of a stone veil

tempered until it becomes impossible to remember this, too
is inert, a rock but not your rock. The most
I knew I knew from their hardened grins,
the ones you get after escaping the inevitable
just long enough to recognize it's still coming.

MAJA LUKIC

August

Gray heat. It's August.
My dead mother's birthday
lodged in the month like a stone.
I have been living
the August of my life for so long,
I remember no other month,
no other kind of pain,
except that for weeks after her death,
I walked in and out of churches across
Lisbon and Sevilla, lighting candles
for her atheist body.
Refusing prayer, refusing closure,
I just wanted to see a light
bloom in the dark
and stay lit among the other candles
standing in the sand.
Then I would step into the bright
heat of the Spanish afternoon,
the slow siesta hours
loud with silence and me
under the orange trees.
In one of the few voicemails
I do have saved,
she is calling me because I fell
asleep with everyone locked
out of the apartment.
She sounds tired
but her love is so clear.
And I sleep, and I sleep.
I keep wanting to wake up
and let her in.

CINDY KING

Anamnesis

I remember the last time I had fish.
It was at a waterfront restaurant
with my mother.
I ordered a cocktail.
My mother brought her own—
a pharmacological rainbow
she shook from what looked to me
like a little plastic coffin.
It was a Saturday or Sunday
when the fish was placed before me,
and when I ran my knife down
the silver length of its body,
it opened its mouth.
Sit up straight, I heard it say,
and *elbows off the table*—
though that was decades ago
and it could have come
from my mother's mouth.
My mother is a fish now, like
the one in the Faulkner novel.
You are what you eat, they say.
I have become a vegetarian
instead of becoming my mother.

TYLER RASO

SHADOW PICTURES—HOW TO ENLARGE OR REDUCE A PICTURE, ETC. [fig. 162 Shadow cast by an Anemone]

after *The American Boy's Handy Book*

Wherever I am, I'm true
only by reference, standing
like a cloth beneath
the thing that names me.
You stare because
you do not expect beauty
from a form like mine.
You stare because
you cannot claim me
in the sand of your
palm. I am with
my anemone everywhere
they go, tucked in
the sweet ache of
their stem until the light
unfolds me like
a forgetting. It's easier
this way. What
would I do with my own
body? Drink sugar
from the well of myself?
Yes, there are things
I wonder about. How it
feels when the dew
settles like stars
creating themselves

in the open dark. How
roots breathe home
into the dirt, into
the rest of you. How
the spring unravels
the promise of yourself
like water flowing
into the arms of water.

HASANTHIKA SIRISENA

Jamais Vu

I HAD BEEN DRIVING THROUGH the strip of rural sex shops for about four years before it occurred to me I wanted to draw it. I'd taken a teaching position at a rural college in Central PA and I spent most of my time trying to escape the area, via the Harrisburg Amtrak station, for New York and Philadelphia. I passed the sex shops and strip clubs on my way to the train. The nondescript concrete-walled blocks remarkable only for the "Girls, Girls, Girls" signage made up a kind of endothelium along this portion of the outskirts of Harrisburg. Hurtling through the membrane at 60 miles per hour felt like a type of piercing, and I could feel the tinge of it on my skin, in my psyche, long after.

I don't think this is prurience on my part. I don't care about porn in any way except that I talk about it in my Queer literature courses, and I teach it seriously because porn is serious. Our culture's lack of meaningful discussion about its production and consumption is even more serious. Porn is a matter of ethics for me, not sex. But my distaste for the strip was, perhaps, in part aesthetic. If you take every bad true crime docuseries, any given season of *Law and Order SVU*, all the midlife crises-turned-crime scenes from *Dateline*, that 1990s David Lynch movie with Laura Dern and Nicolas Cage, fed all this into DALL-E, and asked its artificial neural network to create the schlockiest, most perversely unsexy sex district possible, the strip (and, yes, that is the nickname that locals have given this stretch of highway) would be it. The worst part about the strip isn't what it purports to offer, on the cheap or otherwise. It's that there's so little actual imagination employed.

So, I spent several early mornings and afternoons, over the course of a year, photographing the outside of sex shops. I spent the weekends rendering the photographs, or more specifically, using the governing line, as John Ruskin termed it in his *Elements of Drawing*, that thin, sleek mark I create with a pencil, pen, or stylus, to comprehend the stores, the strip itself, the way the space is being used.

THE GOVERNING LINE, like the straight line, is entirely an invention of human imagination, our yearning to solve problems. Governing lines don't exist in nature. Natural objects, after all, don't come with outlines. Any first year art student can explain to you that a "governing" line, in its simplest craft, workshop definition, is the border between one color and the next. We teach beginning students to use these lines so that they can study proportion, spacial awareness, and perspective. But I wondered one day, after finishing, about three months of steady, daily drawing, why we ever conceived of this. How did our minds invent this process of putting a line around an object to render it, make it recognizable?

According to child developmental studies, we first start using the governing line to "bound" circles at around 3 years. From ages 3–5, children utilize a system of circles, spirals, and scribbles to create mass. This isn't something children are taught. This seems to be something most children naturally do. As a child nears the age of 5, they will start to use a governing line to indicate the trunk of the tree and the branches and scribbles to indicate masses of leaves. In studies conducted by Jean Piaget in the 1950s, very young children were asked to draw glasses containing varying amounts of water. Children younger than 5 used scribbles to indicate water. In other words, if shown half a glass of water, a 3-year old child would draw an outline for the glass and then use scribbles to indicate it was half-filled with water. At about five, the children begin utilizing a single line to indicate the water level.

According to Piaget and the other authors of the study, this doesn't simply represent a moment of observation as much as it's an indication of a new stage in a child's ability to solve problems. Before we understand that that a water line is simply light refracting of water, we know how to solve the problem of it. To paraphrase Rebecca Solnit, the governing line is thought on the page.

Renee Gladman in her artist's book *Prose Architecture* utilizes the governing line in its purest form to render theoretical cities, inventions of her own thought process. She writes:

> . . . I had discovered a new manner of thinking. Drawing extended my being in time; it made things slow. It quieted language. It produced a sense that thinking could and did happen outside of language. I saw the act as a line extending from the body, through the hand, as if being pulled out of one or let go from one. However, in contrast to writing, this line moved in time with thought rather than chasing thought through syntax, as something already over, a moment we can now only describe.

Drawing works in a similar way for me. My mind stops the exhausting whirring and obsessing and eases into some kind of pre-verbal state in which there exists only me and the thing being seen. Drawing focuses me the way that a crossword puzzle does. But a puzzle is about solving someone else's scheme. Drawing, for me, is particular to my own mind. Puzzle and solution are *my* invention.

THE ART CRITIC and teacher John Berger begins the essay "Drawn to the Moment," with a sentence that always gives me pause: "When my father died recently, I did several drawings of him in his coffin." Part of the issue may be that I've long misunderstood who John Berger *is*. I associate him with the 1970s docuseries *The Art of Seeing*. He's an earnest, knowledgeable, articulate guide into this re-thinking of the history of aesthetics, but he a) looks, with his too-long hair and his perhaps slightly too tight shirts and pants, a relic of the Seventies and b) well, I thought he was an art historian. In my entirely anecdotal, very biased experience, art historians are terrible artists. I suspected that the drawings of his father were a kind of a stunt and a slightly ghoulish one at that.

But it turns out I was wrong. Berger was both an art critic *and* an art teacher for over two decades. Specifically, he taught drawing. He is a talented draftsman. And people who draw draw everything just as writers tend to read widely. Also, as a critic, he would have been familiar with the long line of *ars moriendi*, the tradition which includes drawing people on their deathbeds. Still, knowing all this, I can't help but feel a slight aversion to the act of drawing a deceased father.

Drawing is an intimate act. You tend to sit for hours when you draw the human figure following the contours of a face and body with your pencil. When Ruskin first coined the idea of the leading or governing line he meant it by way of instructing the young illustrator of the ability of the line to give form. Anyone who draws portraits knows that the real skill isn't about finding the right proportions but figuring out the small idiosyncrasies of the individual face—the slight downturn in the mouth, the slightly drooping eyelid—that produces a likeness. That takes time and intense focus. Berger describes the process:

> As I drew his mouth, his brows, his eyelids, as their specific forms emerged with lines from the whiteness of the paper, I felt the history and the experience which had made them as they were. His life was now as finite as the rectangle of paper on which I was drawing, but within it, in a way infinitely more mysterious than any drawing, his character and destiny had emerged. I was making a record and his face was already only a record of his life. Each drawing then was nothing but the site of a departure.

However much I might admire the essay as a whole, I can't fully imagine the act he's describing. My father is bedbound and dying now as I write this and I can't imagine going into his room and sitting there and drawing him. *This isn't how I want to remember him*, is the easiest thought that comes to mind. It's closer to the truth to admit that I don't want to spend that much time staring at death.

If Klee is right and the line is "a dot that went for a walk," the governing line is a dot that's gone on a long purposeful walk to contain and articulate. In his essay, Berger goes on to remind us that a century of photography has taught us that the two-dimensional image is static, an act of preservation. But, that's not correct when it comes to a drawing. A drawing is a reminder that looking is subjective and that the act of looking is a series of imperceptible calculations that are as natural, as inborn, as using language.

Berger writes that he has framed one of the drawings of his father and keeps it above his deck. The final line of the essay: *Every day more of my father's life returns to the drawing in front of me.* It's an elegant ending. I also find it to be a very neat ending. He has bounded the grief over his father's death, used the artist's ability of reanimation to give life. But maybe I'm too embroiled in my own grief to be gracious about this. I agree with everything that Berger says about a drawing but I think he misses one final point. A drawing of anything, a flower, a person, a building, unlike a photograph, is more akin to that governing line we discovered at five, the drawn line that indicates a phenomenon that we do not have the mental ability to comprehend but that we can still perceive. A line that makes the unknowing just a little bit closer to the known.

By now, you're probably thinking that I've done no more than reveal an apparently random set of aesthetic boundaries. Drawing crumbling rural sex shops, yes. My dying father, no.

In doing the drawings I realized how much about these shops I hadn't seen. I couldn't sit on the shoulder of the highway or in a gas station parking lot so I drew from photographs taken with an iPhone and photographs distort and blur. I tend not to freehand signage, I measure and use a grid. To make sure I was getting the signs right, I started to Google the billboards . I discovered that the billboards that the sex shops used are generic images bought, or stolen, from the internet. One billboard advertising a strip club depicts a pole dancer. I didn't comprehend until I started drawing it that the woman is fully clothed in a shirt that covers her torso and short leggings. The owners of the strip must have calculated that the largely religious and conservative rural population would tolerate their billboard as long as it didn't actually show a naked woman, and they were right.

A sign in the entrance way of one of the clubs warns "BYOB. No alcohol under 21." Standards. Standards. There are many island fantasy references. The shops are located on a large river island on the edge of the Susquehanna River. I started to research newspaper archives to get a sense of the history of the place. A group of businessmen in the early part of the last decade decided to create a fantasy island in this little part of Central PA. In interviews—the strip club, it turns out, was the focus of intense local media coverage in the middle of the last decade—the owners promise that the strip is going to be tasteful. They don't elaborate so I'm still not sure what they mean.

There's another shop, a small, nondescript cinderblock building with a trailer in the back for peep shows. The trailer is pushed up close to the wall so you can't see anyone walking in between—a nod to privacy. The sign out front declares: Couples Welcome.

My curiosity about what I was looking at so closely led me to discuss the strip with a social worker based in the area and when I mentioned the signs he nodded. He went on to recount an elaborate story of sex rings and wife swapping and even a possible murder. The story was long and sordid and baroque. It's not that I do or don't believe the story. Belief is beside the point. I didn't follow it up, investigate, or verify. The story is entirely hearsay. I am not a journalist in this moment. I'm not even an essayist, really. I'm a person, with a pencil, drawing a governing line.

Over the years, I've spoken to a number of men partly for research, partly out of curiosity, about why they use prostitutes or frequent strip clubs. I don't mean to single out men. Women go to strip clubs. Queer women go to strip clubs. In the Nineties, in New York City, I remember female acquaintances remarking, casually, that they. accompanied their work colleagues to strip clubs in order to celebrate a deal or as part of wooing a client. But, men are, so far, the only ones willing to speak to me about frequenting these clubs. Even though sex shops and strip clubs are populated, managed, sometimes even owned by women, the stigma around frequenting such spaces as a woman is strong.

The reasons men have given me vary and are also often unexpected. One young man was clearly awkward around women in general and struggled in relationships. He told me he thought the women in the strip clubs liked him because he respected their boundaries. Another man told me he frequented prostitutes because he suffered debilitating physical pain and he didn't have to worry about pleasing a prostitute the way he would a sexual partner.

The reasons more often than not leave me feeling a kind of sorrow. Yes, men's sense of privilege when it comes to women's bodies is very much in play. Yes, so is toxic masculinity. But there's often also something else, an after image. Of grief. Of despair. I'm not trying to excuse the behavior. None of the men I spoke to admitted to violence but you go through the reporting on the district and the violence is real and brutal. But, even absolutely acknowledging that, I also think it's wrong to act as if the loneliness and the grief aren't there.

A friend of my girlfriend, a very successful builder, expressed surprise when I told him I was working on these drawings. "You won't like these places. You won't like the people." He went on to explain that he'd been to a number of strip clubs in his career, on business, and they weren't the sort of place for me.

I remembered in that moment, another time, nearly twenty years before, when in a group of friends another man—the husband of a friend of mine—had pointed at me and said, "*She*'s the sort of woman I'd take to a strip club." His wife had just made a quip about wanting to go to a strip club with him, and he had refused. She wouldn't enjoy it, he promised. But when he singled me out, I knew why. I was the only one in the group not partnered. I wasn't out yet—I wasn't even close to sure of myself as a lesbian—but, a few months before, at a party, I'd refused to have sex with a male friend of his and this had gotten out to the group. He pulled back the scrim of politeness and congeniality that bonded us to reveal what they had said about me behind my back. I felt the acid wash of shame but also a hard kernel of resistance. A tight smile. *Sure.*

Like. Dislike. Believe. Disbelieve. I should have told the builder, the friend of my girlfriend, about the governing lines. He works with architects. Maybe then he would have understood.

One of my favorite children's books is *Harold and the Purple Crayon.* It's nearly perfect in its elegance and simplicity. The toddler protagonist, Harold, is rendered as a cartoon figure. The only other illustration is his simple purple crayon drawings that take him physically across landscapes and oceans. In one moment, when he finds himself sinking in the ocean, he draws a boat to rescue him. In another, when Harold finds himself falling off the other side of an unfinished mountain, he draws a hot air balloon to catch him. The governing line becomes both the means for adventure and his salvation.

EARLIER THIS SUMMER, I met the painter Brooke Lanier on a studio tour. Her paintings of long abandoned ships anchored on the Delaware River intrigued me not only for their visual complexity but because they also reduced the ships to angles and sharpened slivers. They weren't miniatures, per se. More like extreme close ups. But they found an intricate, and layered, beauty in the once heroic, now derelict.

But, as much as I liked the painting, I emailed Brooke if she wouldn't mind being interviewed because I really wanted to talk to her about her disability. She wore an eye patch over her right eye and moved in a way—natural and fluid—that made me think the patch was permanent—not the result of an operation or injury. I'm visually impaired in my left eye, so we have this in common: two visual artists who have to negotiate the canvas, and the world this way.

When I returned to the studio a few weeks later, I asked her about the patch. She explained that her doctors had decided a few years back that she should use an eye patch because the right eye was impeding the work of the left. Then she admonished me: "But, I'm not sure I want to focus on that. I don't want people buying my work because I'm a novelty act. I don't want to be reduced to a blind painter."

Brooke is tall, with close-cropped brown hair, and glasses that match her hair color. She's animated when she talks and engaging. She also loves to expound on her work and she's clearly thought through her process and what she wants to accomplish with it. She first spotted the ships through what she describes as peep-holes—gaps in the fencing separating the wharf from the pedestrian walkway. Her first real experience of the ships was piecemeal. That's what inspired the paintings. She ended up spending enough time studying the ships, and talking to the men who worked in the port, to become the first, and I believe up to this point, only artist in residence on one of the abandoned ships, the SS United States.

Ships may be nearly sinking as in Rembrandt's *The Storm on the Sea of the Galilee*, being bombarded as in Manet's *The Battle of the Kearsarge and The Alabama*, or pointed social critiques as in Turner's *The Slave Ship*, but they are also almost always depicted in their entirety—if not heroically, then iconically. But the ships in Brooke's paintings are dissected. Visual artists often set up visual problems for themselves that need to be overcome—depicting light on water is one of them. The water in Brooke's painting shimmers. The ships' hulls appear to be slicing the patterns like razors. Sometimes you can recognize them as the hull of boats. Sometimes you can't. But the act of recognition doesn't seem to be important. What is important is the feeling that you've just stumbled into this moment, just discovered this.

Being sighted in only one eye greatly reduces your stereoscopic vision and, thus, the ability to perceive form in three dimensions. Brooke tells me that as a child she loved to water ski and she learned to assess danger by reading the patterns of light on the water. For example, darker water is deeper. Lighter water is shallower and therefore more dangerous because of possible obstructions. She had similar experiences walking on the street. She studied variations in shadows because it was hard to perceive a break or dip in the sidewalk otherwise.

I ask her if she ever painted people and she laughs. Her voice changes, there's an edge suddenly. "No," she replies firmly. "People don't interest me as subjects. I mean the patterns of their faces. All I see is wrinkles." She pauses and smiles. "And teeth." It occurs to me suddenly what the paintings are about. It's a kind of danger. I mean an artist, with monoscopic vision, navigating the battered, jagged remains of decaying battleships. She's beating down the obstacles with a paintbrush.

Annie Dillard in *Pilgrim at Tinker Creek* writes that, as a child, she loved to draw horses. On a visit to her aunt and uncle's horse ranch, she draws them a horse, to demonstrate. She describes them making gentle fun of her rendering, the lack of any real knowledge of horse anatomy. They then ask her cousins to draw horses. Her cousins, it seems, produce perfectly proportioned horses from memory and Dillard is left with the knowledge that we draw (well) what we love. I don't disagree. But anyone who spends times around horses can tell you that caring for horses is being aware of a constant low-level danger. To stave it off you place your body on theirs almost constantly. Not just when you're astride. A palm on their flank to keep them from kicking you. A hand on their muzzle to pop them if they attempt to bite. Her cousins certainly loved horses but beyond that they also *lived* the horses they worked with. They had to. We draw what we need to know.

IN MY TIME living in Central PA, the strip has come up a surprising amount. At dinner parties with colleagues. In a conversation with a visiting writer. It's mentioned as a blight—a possible hindrance to recruitment since some parents drive through it on their way to visit the campus. I've heard many reasons for it being there. Sex Rings. Drugs. A reaction to an otherwise sexually conservative and oppressive culture. The strip is for truckers. It serves the Amish.

But what surprises me the most when I draw the strip is its aesthetic tentativeness. This isn't 42nd Street in the Seventies. No bright neon lights. No flashing icons of women with gigantic boobs. No posters of muscled men with hard-ons. Yes, the strip promises the lurid, but in the tamest possible way. Last year I taught a late morning workshop in New York City. I woke up at 3:30 in the morning to drive to the train station. I passed one of the strip clubs at 4am and it surprised me to see the place pulsing a bright neon pink and purple, the windows lit up, silhouetted figures moving in and out of the parking lot. It struck me how alive the place suddenly looked. A corpse reanimated. When I drove past the next day, the strip club rested subdued, windows blacked out, underneath a billboard that promised salvation to those who give up their lustful ways. But for all their material solidness, the true aura of these establishments is that of precarity. I want to be careful here because I don't want to appear to be dismissing the real work, and the humanity, of the people in these shops and clubs but the location of these buildings on a remote highway, the disrepair, the invisibility of the people working inside and their clients are all designed to code disposable. For me to continue to fail to see it is a form of collusion.

I don't go to strip clubs and I don't have much interest, anymore, in what's inside sex shops but I think now that I'm drawing them for the same reason that Ed Ruscha makes epic paintings depicting gas stations and motels in the American West. This is the syntax of the world around me. It's my history. This landscape is my America, *our* America.

In "The Work of Art in the Age of Mechanical Reproduction," an essay that is influential on John Berger's own *Ways of Seeing*, Walter Benjamin locates the making, and the reception, of an artwork in ancient ritual. Both Benjamin, and Berger, ascribe to these original artworks a kind of totemic, mystical power, the power of evocation. The guiding line is both elegant solution and lasso for reifying that certain abstract idea which will otherwise elude or evade us. Grief. Fear. The otherwise unbearable. As for my drawings, I've turned some of them into a work of comic journalism. Other sketches remain tucked away in journals and sketchbooks. All these drawings, public or private are mine, of me. And with them, I own, in some way important to me, all that they depict.

Translation Folio

KIM HYESOON

Translator's Introduction

Cindy Juyoung Ok

THE HELL OF THAT STAR writes from within South Korea's violent 1980s military dictatorship. Despite being created and maintained by the U.S., this period in Korean history is a cultural context nonexistent in English language poetry, and heavily redacted even in Korean literature due to the decade's brutal government censorship of art. Kim Hyesoon knew this well working as a literary editor in that period. She was once slapped seven times for refusing to give up the name of one of the authors she published, and she returned home and wrote seven poems in response. Only six of those poems made it to publication, and the specter of that seventh poem (made only of curse words) is present in the book—what is unable to be redeemed and what is required to be remade, what tools are limited by patriarchy and encouraged by isolationism.

In protecting authors, she also had to share the results of the censorship with her authors, which sometimes meant receiving the entirety of a work, including its title and author, covered in tar. Kim experienced this as a death of language and, in another way, a death of the self. When she first gave me her blessing to translate this book, she asked me to convey the voice of the girl, the *sohnyuh*. It is with an intense observance, a mourning awareness, that this voice details turmoil and resistance as experiences, rather than as narrative. Responding to this role as an editor, her own poems initially shrunk and tensed in all ways, struggling to live. State censorship's most catastrophic impact is not on that society's art, but on its artists—the self-censors that begin to live within them, limiting language and thought.

In these poems, "Seeing the Dead Who Came to Eat the Ancestral Offering," "The History of Feed," and "Not Even Knowing He is Dead," ends are considered. What are the logical and sometimes destructive extremes of language and life? Or of desire or death, of physical being alongside visual awareness? Throughout the book, as in such work as an editor, death is not a sudden, momentary threat in this work, but a sustained and ongoing reality to understand and accommodate, much like life. Indeed, these three poems conceive of death in a way that does not oppose it to living, but instead conditions for each reality's confirmation. They declare that accumulating consumption and perception rarely leads to fulfillment. As for Kim, in an essay accompanying the book, she holds that a poet writes with her own ghost, with death; poets are aware of their own absences and existential contingencies, and it is with this relation that the poem can be made.

The poems each address the varied planes of consciousness (in other words, of reality). "큰일 났다," repeats the speaker of "Seeing the Dead Who Came to Eat the Ancestral Offering." The phrase breaks down to mean a big thing has happened, colloquially indicating there has been some trouble, some chaos—an exclamation like "oh shit!" or "huge problem!" But the poem's focus is on what the circumstances seem to be, not just what they are. "The History of Food" ends on the open mouth of an eaten, collapsed mouth, intolerably hungry and accepting a whole ocean at the exact site where the "mother tongue" can be imagined as living. In "Not Even Knowing He is Dead," death is cyclical, flexible, and incidental; the subject continues his monotonous routines, maggots disregarded. The body's strange status as particularly strong but frail, scary or disgusting, is at the core of each poem—what it can withstand, what it must do, always a conscious entity, bound but also unyielding. Much is written and known about how oppressive politics affects girls and women in the towers of empires, but this book has a unique focus on those whose bodies they take as collateral.

In evading censorship, Kim's poems question, twist, and transmute. Outside constructions of sense or story, the book creates, in their wake, a new material with original syntax and estranged diction. Language is a site where the personal and political meet to escape containment, emptiness, and domestication. Her words invoke and abandon structures of masculinity and capitalism as she points to the power of narrative and names to both oppress and liberate, while unable to name those names. The speaker alternates blithe confidence and trembling terror—each masking a national grief, each a performance of humanity and evidence of exile.

KIM HYESOON : Three Poems

Seeing the Dead Who Came to Eat the Ancestral Offering

Me, I see
I can't see and then I see
Me, I see only what is invisible
Me, I don't see what is visible
I see and then I can't see

If I close my eyes, myself buried under
sand is what I see so I know I'm in trouble
If I lie in the bathtub hehe
in the coffin a wide-eyed
me younger than me is what I see
I see the time I was talking to my mother's heart
so I'm in trouble, a huge disaster, trouble that bursts
The dead eating the ancestral offering is what I see
They rush here running
painted seriously in blood and again die
as I see them fall over,
so I'm in big trouble, a serious disaster
Dead *tteuk* on top of my rice bowl
thumping and falling over, I'm in trouble

The History of Feed

—A record of four thousand years of history*

The rail thin woman devours a fat man / She devours him cleanly with not a single toenail leftover / After eating, she keeps looking around to eat again / The more she eats, the skinnier the skinny woman gets / The stick thin woman devours all the fat men and fat women / So fat men and fat women that get eaten become the blood and flesh of the stick thin woman / Hunger leads to hungry blood and hungry flesh that call for hunger / The stick thin hungry woman tries to eat again even after eating everything / Her eyes get bigger and her teeth get sharper / Her hunger gets worse, and the woman can't withstand it, so she cuts up the ground and eats it / Then she cuts off her breasts and eats them and cuts up the rest of her body and eats that too / She also dislodges her pupils and eats them and crunches and munches on her skeleton and eats that / Well, before long now, you shall see the Pacific Ocean hurtling all at once toward the rail thin woman's maw

---

*We who have a four thousand year history of eating people (Lu Xun, *The Diary of a Mad Man*).

Not Even Knowing He Is Dead

Not even knowing he is dead he
gets up in a hurry
Over his empty chest
he gently ties a necktie and
on his dried-out hair
he applies oil and
into the intestines from which maggots crawl
he pours milk and
over his dead feet leather
he puts on leather shoes and
through a street lined with tombstones
he dashes away like the wind

Not even knowing he is dead he
comes back dusting himself off
If he lays a blanket
next to a dead woman's coffin
and bends over

his hair pours and piles up
and cold teeth pour around his mouth
Then, wrinkled skin
falls at his feet and
not even knowing he is dead he
dies again as he
smacks out wonderful
words to be engraved on his tombstone tomorrow and
pulls up the coffin lid himself

—translated from the Korean by Cindy Juyoung Ok

XAVIER BLACKWELL-LIPKIND

The New Face

LOOK: EVERYBODY WAS FORGETTING. I had married a man so severely face blind that he couldn't find me in a hardware store. The neighbors never brought their bins down to the curb on trash day. The barista gave me matcha when I asked for chai. Now I, too, was forgetting. It was September; summer was doing what it could to cover its tracks. On the porch, I read the book for the fourth time, and for the fourth time I forgot it. Not gradually, not in the way that everything is eventually forgotten. My forgetting was immediate. I reached the last page and took in the last sentence, and the instant I closed the book I had no recollection of the characters, the plot, the style. I couldn't even recall whether I had enjoyed it.

This was *The Face*, an anonymous novel published in Occitan in the 1960s that I had been trying to translate for weeks. I sat with it in my lap, the Occitan-English dictionary on one table, the laptop on another. But I couldn't look away without losing my place. I would go to the dictionary and start looking for a word, only to realize that it had escaped me. I would turn to the computer to add a sentence to the document and find myself with nothing to type. All that remained, in these little moments of forgetting, were taunting clues: I had been on page 116 of the novel; I had started to flip toward the back of the dictionary; my fingers hovered over the 'h' key, but for what purpose I didn't know. Hours passed like turned pages.

My face-blind husband came out to the porch and fed me a carrot. He was making soup. This was Thomas, and all he knew was the cello. He played his cello more tenderly than he ever touched me, for which I didn't blame him. The cello was his world, or rather the world was his cello. He saw celli everywhere: in the long faces of bartenders, in the ephemeral formations of migrating geese, in dalmatians, in car windshields, in artichokes. Once he had approached me from behind while I was reading and, mistaking me for an instrument, tried to play Schumann's cello concerto on me, realizing only when I turned to ask what he was doing that I was not made of wood, that my right arm was not a bow. Another time I had caught him flirting with his cello, caressing its spruce body; later he would tell me that he had assumed I was in a quiet mood, or being coy, and that he had attributed the unusual hardness of my skin to goosebumps, or psoriasis, or both.

Thomas asked whether I was making any progress on the translation.

"No," I said, rubbing my eyes. "It's almost as if it doesn't want to be translated. It's resisting its own recognition."

"Soup will be ready in fifteen. You can take a break from Occitan and come burn your tongue like last time."

"I've told you what I do with my tongue when I'm translating, right?" I knew that I hadn't, but I liked to pretend that I was worried about repeating myself. The truth was that I never said the same thing twice. I couldn't, even if I tried. I just couldn't: my eyes would tear up; I would get a tickle in my throat. The words would hide, afraid to be reused. As if to say: *once*.

"I don't think you've ever told me," Thomas said. "What, do you bite it?"

"I run it across my palate, over and over. In the same direction, at the same speed. Front to back." Translation was all about tongues. Mine ended up going raw from the neverendingness of this front-to-back motion, the againstness of it.

As I agonized over *The Face* and its inscrutable contents, the inside of my mouth had become a conveyor belt, numb and self-sustaining, the tongue completing its semiconscious cycles. I was reminded of the baggage carousel at the local airport, the way people always stood there waiting: the flash of excitement in their eyes at a bag that might be theirs but wasn't, the alarm signaling the arrival of new luggage, the childlike glee provoked by this sound in even the most serious adults, the inherent comfort of stuff, of the mere promise of stuff, of promises—IOUs, I wills, soons, somedays, lies.

There was something peculiar about this process, something incestuous. To be human was to be a bag, to hold and be held. One stood in the carpeted basement of the airport and waited for oneself to emerge on the belt, then, seeing oneself at last, seized one's handle or clutched one's strap and ran, hailing a cab or finding a bus or catching a train and vanishing into a city of more belts and conveyances. In airports, one anticipated oneself.

Thomas grimaced. I had nearly forgotten that he was standing next to me, glasses halfway down his nose, or maybe nose halfway up his glasses, though that made no sense. "Are you doing that right now?" he asked. "With your tongue?"

"No. Because I'm not translating. I'm talking to you. But once you go back to the kitchen, it'll start back up."

"I kind of wish you hadn't told me this."

He was serious, I could tell, but I laughed. There was a piece of carrot stuck between my two front teeth now. It felt like a little orange wedge had been driven into me. Thomas went inside to check on the soup, and I sat and stared at the book and hated it, which wasn't fair. My tongue traced its sullen line. I read a sentence and forgot it. All that remained was a sense that I had once known it. An almost-rememberable dream, a piece of music recognized but not identified.

The soup was good. All the best soups, I decided, stuck with you. You woke up with the taste still in your mouth. You spent the next day unable to rid yourself of the memory of the chicken broth, a memory so tangible that it turned into a sort of broth itself. You licked at it; it went nowhere. Books sat on tables; tables sat on porches; porches sat. Everybody was forgetting, and everything was being forgotten, but there was always the soup.

•

THE ORCHESTRA IN which Thomas played as assistant principal cellist boasted several homosexual woodwind players. The first clarinetist had hit on him four years back, the piccoloist a year before that. Both times Thomas had politely said no, and that had been that. The principal oboist, Griffin, was a more complicated case. Griffin knew Thomas was face blind. More precisely, Griffin knew Thomas was so face blind that he would be incapable of distinguishing his husband from an oboist. I had met him after a Mahler-themed concert a few months back. "Your husband," he told me in the lobby, "is a great guy. You're very lucky to have him. If I cared a little less about right and wrong, I'd study your mannerisms and trick him into thinking that I was you." I forced a smile, and Griffin copied it. That night, I had opened a blank Word document, typed "I do not trust double reeds," and dragged the file into the trash.

Sometimes I presented these scenarios to Thomas as pure hypotheticals. "What if," I would ask him in bed, "somebody made you believe that they were me?"

And Thomas would say, "I would never let that happen."

But I worried. I was plagued by a vivid dream in which a man dragged me from my own house and took my place at the dinner table. Thomas grinned and chatted the whole time, unaware that one man was being replaced by another. I barged back into the house, and Thomas, unable to recognize me, called the police. I had become the impostor, the imitator, the non-husband.

We got Italian takeout on a Tuesday. Thomas played A Flock of Seagulls on the gray Bluetooth speaker that we had named Martha. Every few songs, an ad would interrupt the music: a horror movie with a faceless villain; cataract surgery; a home security system with infrared cameras; a hypnotherapist specializing in social anxiety disorders and intrusive thoughts. I burned my cheek on the gnocchi. We agreed to turn off Martha for the night. The house was quiet but not silent. The kitchen smelled like mozzarella. I didn't want the kitchen to smell like mozzarella; I wanted the kitchen to smell like a kitchen. We talked about thesauri and "Space Age Love Song" and the principal violist's new nose ring, and the conversation was good and fresh, like cheese. There came a point about halfway through the gnocchi when there was something I wanted to say but couldn't remember.

"Damn it," I said.

"What?"

"I was going to say something."

"It's gone?"

"Not quite. It's lingering. Right where I can't see it."

"Why not just let it go?"

"Do you want me to let it go?"

"I've just learned not to lose sleep about the things I can't call up, that's all. Faces, mostly."

When I told Thomas that nothing scared me more than forgetting, missing the things around and behind me, letting the words I wanted to say become words I could have said, leaving the past to be the past, separating myself from what came before—when I explained, in bed or in the kitchen or in the car, that the frustration I experienced when I couldn't remember what I wanted to say was unlike any pain I had experienced, that it faded but never disappeared, that it came back, sharp and existential, to prod me while I was in line or at a red light, to remind me that it had been forgotten—when I took notes on my phone about everything happening around me, recording in painstaking detail the number of tissues remaining in the box or the color of the squirrel on the porch or the time at which the garbage truck came on Wednesday—Thomas looked at me as if to say, "You are an anomaly," as if to say, "All the real humans know how to forget," to say, "The more I confuse your face with my cello, the more of a person I will be." So I had mostly stopped telling Thomas that nothing scared me more than forgetting.

"Am I supposed to believe," I said, mouth still fat with gnocchi, "that you would rather forget everything than remember everything?"

"Absolutely," he said. There was no hesitation, no new paragraph, no enter and tab. This was not a question that required thought. It was a question so obvious as to be preceded by its answer.

"Why's that?"

"I've spent my whole life almost remembering faces. I promise there's nothing worse than that *almost*."

"But that's exactly why remembering everything seems to me like the better choice. You know, there's that instant where you have something, you're practically holding it, and suddenly all that's left is the knowledge of an absence, the knowledge that something was once there. Wouldn't it be nice to do away with all that uncertainty? To hold things and know that they're not going anywhere?"

"I don't know. Being unable to forget sounds like hell to me, but I don't know if I can articulate why. Maybe a part of me has come to enjoy moving through the world and not retaining certain information. It gives me space to doubt. And to leave things behind. People."

I took out my phone and, in the Notes app, wrote, "space to doubt and to leave things behind."

"See?" Thomas said.

"What?"

"There's always more to record. You can't spend your whole life recording."

"I'm a translator, aren't I?"

"You create things when you translate."

"By recording them."

He sighed. "I love you, Leo." It sounded like he meant it.

In bed, Thomas read Proust in English. I held *The Face*. I didn't try to read it. I just held it. It felt like a book, like something that wanted to be remembered. It had weight, and corners, and it carried the odor of all the other books it had touched in the shop in Marseille where I'd found it a few years ago, books crumbling, books thin, books bent, books untranslated. The old man had charged me four euros. "A good choice," he told me. "Thank you," I said, pretending to believe that he had read the book, or even heard of it.

Thomas set down his book and switched off the lamp on his side of the bed and turned to face me. He was looking at me, waiting for me to say something. Expecting a conversation. Instead I set down my book and switched off the lamp on my side of the bed. There was no malice in this choice, which Thomas knew as well as I did. There was simply nothing to say. Our marriage was sharp cheddar, not cottage cheese. We talked when we talked. Everything delineated, the edges hard. We liked it that way.

When I turned out the light, there was that almost-magical moment in which the room ceased to exist—until it began, as it always did, to gently reassert itself, the bathroom door tracing itself in gray, the line of light on the ceiling begging to be noticed, Thomas's sloped body saying, "I'm here," until all I could do was see, see what had been and then had not been and now was again, see and see until I wanted to remember existing without eyes, before eyes, existing in a bag inside my mother, until I wanted a greater darkness, a more perfect darkness. But there was no such thing.

I dreamed of Thomas calling me Griffin. I dreamed that I knew how to play the oboe and that Griffin could speak Occitan. I dreamed that I couldn't remember that I was not Griffin. I dreamed that Thomas couldn't remember that I was not Griffin. I woke up early and opened the Notes app and wrote, "You speak Occitan, you do not play the oboe," over and over until my thumb cramped up and I went into the bathroom to shave.

•

GRIFFIN INVITED US to dinner. Thomas said yes on our behalf. I told Thomas that this was a mistake. I told Thomas that I didn't trust Griffin. Thomas told me not to worry.

"Griffin," he said, "is just an oboist."

I wasn't sure what that was supposed to mean, so I just stood there, in the upstairs bathroom, like a plane waiting at a gate.

"You have the least forgettable face I have ever seen," he said.

I ran my tongue, front to back, across my palate. "Okay," I said, "turn around."

"What?"

"Just turn around."

He was facing the wall now, and I was facing his back, and behind us was an open door, and through that door the stairs, and to our right the shower where we had once tried to have sex and vowed never to try again, and to our left the mirror, in whose glass I could see the side of Thomas's neck, which was smooth except for a small pimple peeking out over the collar of his shirt. I looked at him for a minute, looked at him as he looked at the wall, and said, finally, "Tell me what I look like."

"What?"

"Don't turn around. Describe me."

"Leo."

"Do I have the least forgettable face you have ever seen?"

"Of course you do."

"So tell me what it looks like."

"This isn't fair."

"What color are my eyes?"

There was a long silence. I had something I wanted to say, something biting, something like, "That's what I thought," but not that, something else. I wasn't sure. So I said nothing and left the bathroom and ran down the stairs, Thomas's "I'm sorry" missing me by meters, and went for a walk with my face. I passed the cemetery and the cathedral and the triangular park and the corner store, and I thought, it's a nice day, isn't it, the air feels right on my hands, and the sidewalk wants me on it, and I have a nose, and everything smells like pomegranate, what a nice day, I will call the only person ever to publish a translation of *The Face*. And I did.

Her name was Apolline Martin, and she had completed a French translation two years before. Her book—her face—told the simple story of a man and the things he loved: the tissues with which he blew his nose, the leash with which he walked his dog, the pen with which he wrote letters to his son—all those *with whiches* that traced the quiet contours of his life. It was not a book I found myself struggling to remember. We had exchanged some emails, and she had encouraged me to call at any time, but it was never clear to me whether people meant that. The phone rang; she picked up; I told her who I was; she sighed. That, I figured, was my answer.

"I'm so sorry," she said, "but it's not a great time. My mother has Alzheimer's, and she's just forgotten my father's name for the first time, and he's a wreck. I'm on the train to go see them."

"No, no," I said, "I'm so sorry." I wanted to feel more than I did. I was good at this: convincing myself that the world was far from me, alienating myself from so many things that I ended up alienating myself from my own alienation.

"I can answer a quick question, if that's all you have. I'm just a little out of it."

"Of course. That's all I have. Just a quick question." Yes, I was a brilliant alienator. As I circled back to the triangular park and sat on a bench with a dead person's name on it, I thought, I am easily the best alienator in this entire city. I explained to Apolline that I couldn't seem to remember *The Face*, no matter how hard I tried. I told her that the verbs always slipped my mind, and with the verbs went the nouns, and with the nouns the adjectives, and with the adjectives the adverbs, and all that remained were small words that by themselves meant nothing: an, if, on. I asked Apolline how she had managed not to forget the book each time she closed it.

There was a pause. I could hear the train in the background, its engine rumbling like a slow roll on a bass drum. "Who says I remembered it?" she asked finally.

"What do you mean?"

"This is not a book that wants to be remembered, Leo. That gives you the unique opportunity as a translator to write whatever you want. If the text leaves you with nothing, if it leaves you entirely alone, dropping its prepositions behind it like a leaky engine—if you have nothing to translate, anything you write is a translation."

"Wouldn't it be that nothing I write is a translation?" There was a melody coming from around the corner, quiet, barely audible. I recognized it from a wind quintet Thomas had introduced me to. A clarinetist, busking, perhaps, or an oboist.

"Nobody is ever going to be able to evaluate the accuracy with which you've translated this manuscript. That's all I'm saying. You'll be remembered based on what you write. What you invent."

"So should I read it again?"

"What's the point?" she asked. "I mean, what is the point? Why do something you know you'll forget?"

In the Notes app, I typed, "What is the point?"

I was in a triangle, but the triangle was in a place of many squares. The city unfolded like a piece of graph paper, flat and rigid. Blocks met blocks; people lived in block-shaped buildings and looked out over the blocks through block windows and thought, how lucky I am to see such gorgeous blocks from my block of an apartment. This was why I liked the park: it was an interruption, a distortion of the four-sidedness of it all. When I was in the park, I didn't feel as much as I normally did that my life was a series of unrelated, blink-sliced moments. I peeled myself off the graph paper.

"Is that wrong?" I asked finally. "To do that?"

"My mother doesn't know who her husband is," she said. "That's wrong. This is art. Art can be bad, or ugly, or derivative, but it's rarely wrong."

"I'm not sure I agree," I said. "I think art is wrong all the time."

"No," she said, "that's wrong."

We said goodbye. I wandered over to the corner store and bought a bag of mini muffins, which seemed like an appropriately sullen food. I walked east and opened the bag and began to pick the muffins out with two fingers. They were so small. It was ridiculous. Years before, at the airport, waiting for a flight to Marseille, I had bought a bag of similarly miniscule muffins and eaten them at the gate. Eating those muffins, I had been overwhelmed by a sense of aloneness. I was a man in an airport eating tiny muffins; everybody around me was a stranger; there were only the muffins and the bags, the bags everywhere, dragged and toted and left outside bathrooms and unzipped and rezipped and holding and held and bulging with motion sickness remedies and changes of clothes and magazines bought to be left unread. And I had said to myself, "Here is something close to living. The pastries too small, the planes too large, the lights too strong, everybody looking elsewhere." My mouth tasted like blueberry and dough. Layers of flour accumulated until there was scarcely room for me to breathe. I ran my tongue across my palate, front to back. A man announced on the intercom that the flight to Marseille had been delayed. His voice sounded like that of an old friend pretending to recognize me at a college reunion. He provided neither an explanation for the delay nor an estimate of its length. So I bought another bag of mini muffins. And ate it, and bought another. By the time I boarded, I had gone through seven of those bags. I vomited the whole way to France; the stuff was blue and came out in fits, one little muffin at a time. Now I was waiting again, but not for a plane. I was waiting for the book to let me remember it and for Thomas to recognize me. I was waiting, in short, for a series of small impossibilities. I walked east until the bag was empty, then turned and retraced my steps, then walked east again. It went on for hours.

At one point, near the laundromat, I caught sight of a man across the street. He was standing still, watching me, right hand clutching what looked like an oboe case. I saw the figure again forty minutes later, outside the Thai place where Thomas and I always ordered green curry and got red. I ignored the man. There were plenty of men in the city, many of them watching other men, many of them holding things in their hands.

But I recognized the man, and the man recognized me.

•

GRIFFIN'S HOUSE WAS small, and when we walked in the television was on. It was tuned to one of those stations that played only infomercials. Griffin was thin as a reed; he wore jeans and a red hoodie and glasses. I, too, wore jeans and a red hoodie and glasses. I felt sick, but I smiled, which I was good at.

"Hi," I said.

"Hi," Griffin said, "so good to see you again. Let me turn this off." The pitch of his voice matched mine exactly. Before he switched off the television, I overheard a woman talking about the new face of cleaning. I had always found it strange that ads talked about the new faces of things. As if one face were being replaced by another. As if the old face were being torn away from its body.

The three of us sat at a round table with three white napkins and three white bowls and three sets of silverware and a vase in the middle with a single iris. "I'm so glad we were finally able to do this," Thomas said.

"Me, too," Griffin and I said at the same time. Griffin looked over at me and raised his eyebrows, then took off his glasses and flicked away a lash that had been trapped under the bridge. I watched him like an old video of myself.

"Can I offer you some salad?" he asked.

The first time I saw Thomas, he was performing with his string quartet in a small recital space. I was twenty-four and he was twenty-six. They were playing Borodin's second quartet, which I had loved since I was seven. The piece began with a soaring melody in the cello. I watched Thomas finger the first minor third and land on the high A with a shiver of vibrato. I wasn't somebody who did much crying, but by the fifth measure I was almost there. The piece unfolded like a map; it was less a line than it was a space, something you couldn't trace. I was *in* it; it was *around* me. The harmonies seemed to exist beyond time. They twisted around themselves, traveled forward and backward in the same breath. I kept my eyes fixed on the cellist the whole time. It wasn't that I found him attractive. It was that he sat at the center of the most beautiful thing I could remember experiencing in years. He was an embodiment of the sounds he was creating. He was music physicalized. He was the cello. I forgot everything else. It was terrifying.

After the recital, I had walked up to Thomas and said, "Your cello is lucky to have you." I didn't walk up to people very often, and when I did, I certainly didn't say things like that.

"Thank you," he said. He talked slowly, carefully, like a bow being drawn across a string.

We went to a club. He had to use the bathroom, so he left me at the bar, and when he came back I was waiting for him on the dance floor, but he couldn't find me. They were playing Eurythmics, or a cover, or a cover of a cover. Thomas had just stood there, turning around, making half-circles with his feet, scanning the faces in the dark, hoping for an eye or a lip or an ear, something he could latch onto, something he could remember. When I finally walked up to him and took his hand and led him onto the floor, he looked at me as if he were seeing me for the first time. That had been my first exposure to the notion that it was possible to know someone and to meet them again and again. I didn't understand at the time that I would need to be reintroduced to this man thousands of times over the next few months: at restaurants and at weddings, in buses and in bed, before and after concerts. All I understood was that he was nice and funny, and he played the cello naturally, instinctively, like he was blinking his own eyes, and I wanted him to like me. And he did.

That was the first time I saw Thomas, and the first of many first times he saw me. I was to learn that Thomas lived life in firsts. That the only seconds and thirds he knew were those he played on the cello.

Griffin brought my bowl back. It was filled to the brim with salad. "There you are, Griffin," he said, setting it down in front of me.

"I'm Leo," I said.

"Right. I'm sorry."

Soon we all had our salads. I asked Thomas what he thought about spinach.

"I'm a fan," he said. "Yeah, you could call me a fan of spinach." We laughed, the three of us.

"I'm glad," Griffin said, "because that's all I've got. Oboists don't make enough for arugula."

"*Principal* oboists," Thomas said. Griffin's red hoodie was the same size and color as mine. It was the same as mine.

I said, "Do you have anything to drink?"

Griffin grinned. I hadn't seen him grin like that before. "Of course," he said. He disappeared through a doorway.

I turned to Thomas. "I'm nervous," I said.

"Don't be." He was looking at me in that funny way. Like I was new to him. It was another first time.

Griffin emerged through a different doorway with two large bottles of red wine and three wine glasses; after placing the bottles in the middle of the table, on either side of the iris, he set the glasses behind our bowls with a precision that frightened me. He opened the first bottle and poured us all the same amount of wine. "Cheers," he said.

Thomas raised his glass. "A toast," he said, "to the musicians of the world, and to the translators of the world, and to all the people who remember and forget." I thought that was a bit sentimental as toasts went, but I held my tongue. Thomas touched his glass to Griffin's. Then Griffin touched his glass to mine. Then I touched my glass to Thomas's. They were looking at each other.

We finished the salad and the bottle. The wine pushed itself through me; I felt a pressure rising to my head. I imagined that I was in a landing plane, and that I had stolen everybody's complimentary pretzels and was eating them so fast that I was running out of room in my body, and that we had to abort the final approach and try a second time, and that the flight attendants all had the same face, and that the pretzels filled me up and burst through my skin, and I was just a heap of pretzels on the floor of a landing plane, and the same-faced flight attendants came to clean me up, and I was gone.

Griffin was talking. "They've performed several successful face transplants," he said. "You know, after catastrophic accidents. Fires, car crashes. They put the new face on, they attach it at the edges and drape it over the cartilage in the nose, and over time the face comes to look like a face. It finds its shape."

"I wouldn't want that," I said.

Griffin turned to me. "Why not, Griffin?" he asked.

"I wouldn't want to look in the mirror and see somebody I didn't recognize," I said. I didn't say, "My name is Leo." I didn't say, "You are calling me by the wrong name, and I know why." He was trying to play a strange game with me, a sort of musical chairs of identity, but I was tired now, and drunk, and I let him call me Griffin. I was willing to let him win if it meant leaving earlier, getting home earlier, ending up in bed with my husband earlier, turning to him in the dark and looking at the shape of his body under the blanket and committing it to memory.

"That," Thomas said, "is what I see every time I look in the mirror. Somebody I don't recognize."

"Oh, honey," Griffin said, taking Thomas's hands.

"God, Leo," Thomas said, staring at Griffin, "you look like a cello."

•

I HAD READ an article, years before, about a car accident. There was one woman in a green sedan; there were two women in a gray hatchback. They crashed at an intersection late at night, and the woman in the sedan died. The women from the hatchback, panicking, found that the doors to the sedan were unlocked, so they took the body and buried it. And then one of the women from the hatchback slid into the front seat of the sedan and called the police. They had only minor injuries, and they pretended not to have known each other before the accident. It worked, it all worked, until the mother of the woman in the sedan came looking. She saw a photograph of the woman whom the police had found in the sedan and said, in so many words, "That is not my daughter." But almost. It almost worked.

Thomas and Griffin went home and left me in Griffin's house. "Goodnight, Griffin," they told me.

I didn't try to stop them. I wanted to sleep. "Goodnight, Thomas," I said. "Goodnight, Leo." I curled up on the couch and thought about the two of them in my bed. What would they be up to? Griffin would be setting his glasses on the bedside table. I could see it. And as I watched him set his glasses on the bedside table, his face shadowy, I could almost convince myself that he was me, or rather that I was him, that I was the oboist, that I had projected myself through these walls and down these streets and around these corners and was back in bed with the cellist: the cellist draping an arm over the oboist, the cellist whispering something to the oboist, the cellist laughing with the oboist before, at last, we fell asleep, two musicians, unremembering and unrecognizing and in love.

I woke up early with a headache and an idea. I had left my laptop at the house; I would get it later. In the meantime, I found a pad of paper on one of many music stands and grabbed a pen from the desk in the corner and began to write. "Bags," the first sentence read, "are the atoms of the airport." This was *The Face*. My face. I was translating from nothing. I wrote so fast the ink began to lag behind itself, so fast, impossibly fast, the ideas running after their own expressions, the words trying to remember themselves; I wrote so fast, so mercifully, mercilessly fast, that I didn't have time to think that Thomas's face blindness wasn't enough, that Griffin's red hoodie wasn't enough, that my husband knew, that my husband had made a choice, that we weren't going back; I wrote so fast that it all became slow again; I wrote about little boys losing themselves in the cavernous halls of airports, screens announcing the arrivals and departures of aircraft and thus of people, music playing in the many-stalled bathrooms, families divided throughout and across planes, faces alone at the windows, hands pushing the shades all the way up for takeoff, as if seeing what one was leaving behind would make one safer, as if one could watch the past from the sky. I wrote until I was done, until the roof of my mouth stung, until the pen was dead.

Look: I don't remember what I did after that. I might have put down the notepad and walked to the triangular park and sat on a bench. I might have called one of the hypnotists I had heard about in the ads the speaker played between songs and asked him to make me forget every face I had ever seen. I might have signed up for oboe lessons. I might have gone to confront Thomas and been greeted by a man who had forgotten, who had no idea who I was, who threatened to call the police if I didn't leave his property, who looked at me as if I had gone at his cello with a baseball bat. I might have gone at his cello with a baseball bat. What I do know is that, at some point, hours or days or weeks later, I bought a bag of mini muffins. And I ate those muffins, alone, in the house that was beginning to feel like it was mine. They were tiny. They were so tiny. In the Notes app, I wrote, "so small, so small, the muffins, like castanets, like model airplanes, each muffin a time-eroded memory of itself." I counted them. There were sixteen. That was enough.

MYA MATTEO ALEXICE

Taekwondo Lesson

we take | Taekwondo | twice a week | we say | hana | dhul | trap it under the western roof of our mouths | we say hannah | duel | we bow to the flags | master ▮▮▮▮ uses gorilla to describe men we should avoid on the street | tells us to practice self-defense | in high school my mixed martial arts sensei [there's a joke about being mixed there | but we've done that one before] uses the word immigrant | to describe men we should avoid on the street | I walk out of class but go back next week | my mother has already paid for the month | master ▮▮▮▮ laughs off police brutality | he used to be a cop, you see | used the art of Taekwondo to backfist | a community | to enforce | force | we bow at the waist | he keeps using the black and brown men | in class | as examples. listen, what would you do if ▮▮▮▮ was coming toward you at night? elbow to the throat, sweep the leg | yes, sir | gamsa-hamnida |

and now I find myself halfway to my black belt |

[there's a joke about being half-black there | but we've done that one before]

in Taekwondo the black of a belt means ultimate | knowledge | white is virgin | ignorant | desperate to be colored in | year after year until obsidian is all that remains | the darkness beyond the sun itself | in Taekwondo black

is an honor | with every extension
of my pivoted hip,
I am rising and darkening
and becoming more
and more

whole | we culturally exchange | right? we appropriate | right? I'm sorry we took | a culture and used it | to fight | amongst ourselves | I bow to masters | & sometimes they bow back.

MARK HALLIDAY

Enough Some Day

Each day I feel something is missing but maybe
on a day when I'm eighty-seven I'll have a beautiful moment
of accepting mortality, the ending of me,
I'll feel the radiance of acceptance giving me a glow of wisdom
that others will admire
if anyone is around to notice;

suffused will be the word for my condition, I'll be suffused
with awareness of my hardly credible decades of good luck
and the word *enough* will become so blossomy with meaning
and maybe I'll murmur *Cela suffit*
to add a Euro-dollop to my radiance

and I'll reread some barely remembered poem
found somewhere amid the overloaded bookshelves
(those shelves loaded with did-I-try-hard-enough until that day)—
it might be "Let That Be Plenty" by Laure-Anne Bosselaar
in her book *These Many Rooms*
and my understanding of the poem just then will be unlimited
unlike my life.

MATTHEW NIENOW

Useless Prayer

After the night & its empty bottles, Lord, brown glass
in a paper bag, the music of breaking

like the voices of angels, un-
intelligible, I fold my hands together in the sign

of prayer & begin, *O Lord of how-time-flies*
swatting days down from the calendar, each

day drawn like a cell & with bars to keep
who's boss known, Lord of the sour stomach

& slow walk to the grease joint burger stand
to get a dose of dopamine, my brain in sync

with the flickering fluorescents in the gas station
coolers, the beer just below room temp—

O Lord of my last dollar, I need a longer drink.
I'd close my eyes for good, Lord,

but someone has been tampering with the dark

It Could Be That My Heart Was Not in It

When winter crosses over the field & ten

thousand shards of ice trap a glint of dawn

in their shields, I cannot

say I would have rather made a life

from money, hiring the house built,

while long hours away earned a wealth

our country says I should want.

Curator of the Intangible, Little Thief

of Whispers Hiding in Plain Sight

are names I give myself. I pay

attention to everything. What is it called

when the cure lives within the curse?

JAMES JABAR

Bobo the River Boy Sings at the Bottom of the Tallahatchie for Bodies No. 7 & 8

They come in soundless, their last words trapped in a million
bubbles that form around the skull like a cocoon

their heads turning so fast, from left to right, to read
every last thought, I thought their necks would unscrew

from their shoulders   *No*. They come in nameless & searching
for direction their heads turning so quickly, from east to west,

trying to find the sun (the Tallahatchie can be so dark here
at the bottom) the soles of their feet dragged here by an engine block

where most are buried forever & they were scared when they saw
me, stayed inside their floating shells peeking out the windows

of the eyes, flung open & glazed over, to see if I was real before exiting
through the mouth. They stood beside me & each held my hands

as we watched the Garra rufa prepare the bodies; close the eyelids
reconnect the lips so that they could not reenter & when it was done

I carried them over to kiss themselves goodbye for most traveled down
to the Yazoo in search of heaven but they decided to wait; wait for arrival,

wait for discovery, wait for ascension until their patience was rewarded
their bodies pulled to the surface with 6 more & so they kissed me & let go

of my hands to grab onto their own & evaporated into the ripples of light
at the surface. & I remember the remnants of myself & its departure

from the water, when I reached out to grab my mangled fingers & looked
into an unrecognizable face & pulled back; reminded of how the open air

up there can do so much wonder   *No.* cause so much damage to the body

EMILY CINQUEMANI

Poem for the Archeologist Excavating My Remains

At the dig site—your head lost in a morning's conversation
or lover's touch or next meal—you reveal me from the ground
and I'm taken whole to a museum, kept in soft light and a glass
box: *21st century woman.* You herd my swarm of worry

into the width of a century, my decade's violence a line
of text beside the fact that it was customary for someone
like me to have soup for dinner, eaten with an instrument
called *spoon.* I like imagining your categories, my skeleton

clean and tucked into a numbered drawer. Here, I am only
part of a whole. In your hands, a series of answers:
height and race, a right arm re-healed. You know my age
of death, whether or not my pelvis is marked with the trauma

of childbirth. You know my society and ancestry, which articles
refer to as *my belonging,* though you too must know it's not so simple
as relative and religion, as dirt under your feet. I've moved
back to the town where I was born, wake up under the same sun

that woke everyone in every time on earth, drink coffee,
but if I reach back even a few years the woman there's obscured
by dust, sinking deeper into the earth of my memory. Do you
ever dream your life into an equation with a solution, grow tired

of building a moat to combat an internal invasion? I shouldn't
have slid God into a desk drawer without a back. When I turn
my soul over it crawls out of sync, has millions of bug legs. Some days
I'm a character from my own daydream, and I worry I'll snap out

of my life to find myself back in a classroom at sixteen. I can't
tell you what comes next, give you any hard data, say this is a sign
of the times or of growing older. Tonight, I drive to my childhood
house for dinner, down roads so memorized I forget them

along the way. My family watches stories where travelers
navigate space in another century. From the window, small
as votive candles, distant headlights float their way home.
We sit together in a big room, cook dinner on the stove.

CHRIS FORHAN

In the Funny Pages

Of infancy, I recall crosshatched shadows, my thoughts punctuation marks in balloons above my head. After I learned to talk I was not inclined to, unless it meant chatting with my dark-eyed Dondi doll, a cartoon orphan, my black-haired twin, a waif imagined into being by Gus Edson, a real man who, being real, was dying then, in 1966, though I couldn't have known that, couldn't have guessed he might be gasping a last breath as I was kissing his creation's plastic forehead.

Gus made an actual boy, too: Russell—named to bind father and son in rhyme. Gus and Russ. My own dad (I had one) was rarely there, a stock peripheral character, drawn always in hat and tie, hand on an adding machine or the wheel of the family sedan. He vanished, at last, for good. I couldn't: one panel, one page, gave way to another, then another—always, no matter how clipped or trivial the events, I was at the center of them.

Decades later, my doll gone, my dad in a cloud, I found the poems of Russell Edson, Gus' boy, grown now: cartoonish dream-drenched dramas of sea captains, talking hogs, eggs, and men befuddled into loneliness. Fathers, in other words.

That's what I noticed, anyway. Fathers all through those poems.

GEOFFREY BROCK

The Makers

after Heather McHugh's "Fable"

The children are the makers of the parents,
by cut and paste, by drag and drop, by trial
and terror. Out of a drawer of craft supplies
come monsters and self-portraits, come blue torrents
descending from gray cliffs and pooling while
glue dries on cotton clouds. Beneath such skies,

two larger figures stand beside two smaller
against a field of green, hands fused, heads sprouting
sunflower petals. A trail of seeds (or breadcrumbs?)
leads to the right, toward forests of no color.
And not till sun turns into moon and the trotting
cow in the pasture on the left becomes

these burgers on the grill do lullabies
get sung, their black notes weaving up like bats
to fashion night. And not till children sleep
does a house grow up around them, swelling in size,
filling with windows made of scissored bits
of landscape, in which yellowhammers keep

tacking the lawn in place. Then yellow buses
appear and children vanish, leaving their art
unfinished. And not until they too are grown
and shrinking slowly as mortgage balances
to fit new parts they'll never learn by heart
may children lay their parent bodies down.

Bios

ANTHONY M. ABBORENO teaches at Eastern Iowa Community Colleges. His stories appear in *American Short Fiction, Outlook Springs*, and *Planet Scumm*.

Originally from Pennsylvania, ALLISON ADAIR teaches at Boston College. She is the author of *The Clearing* (Milkweed, 2020), winner of the Max Ritvo Poetry Prize. Her poems appear in *Best American Poetry, The Kenyon Review, The Threepenny Review, Zyzzyva*, and elsewhere. She has received a Pushcart Prize, the *Florida Review* Editors' Award, and the Orlando Prize.

MYA MATTEO ALEXICE's debut poetry collection *A Shape We've Yet to Name* is forthcoming from Game Over Books in March, 2024. Their poems appear in *The Bennington Review, Barrelhouse, Hayden's Ferry Review, The Pinch,* and elsewhere. They work at the New York Public Library.

Dominican American poet and educator DIANNELY ANTIGUA was born and raised in Massachusetts and is currently the Poet Laureate of Portsmouth, New Hampshire. Her debut collection *Ugly Music* (YesYes, 2019) won the Pamet River Prize and a 2020 Whiting Award. Her second poetry collection, *Good Monster*, is forthcoming from Copper Canyon in 2024. Her poems appears in *The American Poetry Review, Poem-a-Day, Poetry, Washington Square Review*, and elsewhere.

RICK BAROT's most recent book of poems, *The Galleons*, was published by Milkweed Editions in 2020 and was longlisted for the National Book Award. His work has appeared in *The Kenyon Review, The New Republic, The New Yorker, Poetry*, and elsewhere, and he has received fellowships from the Guggenheim Foundation, the National Endowment for the Arts, and Stanford University. He lives in Tacoma, Washington, and directs The Rainier Writing Workshop, the low-residency MFA at Pacific Lutheran University.

JAN BEATTY's new book, *Dragstripping*, is forthcoming from the University of Pittsburgh Press in 2024. Recent books are a memoir, *American Bastard* (Red Hen, 2021), and a poetry collection, *The Body Wars* (Pittsburgh, 2020). Beatty has worked as a waitress, an abortion counselor, and in maximum security prisons. She is Professor Emerita at Carlow University, where she was Distinguished Writers in Residence of the MFA Program.

XAVIER BLACKWELL-LIPKIND studies comparative literature at Yale and serves as editor-in-chief of *The Yale Literary Magazine*. His work appears in *Gulf Coast, The Threepenny Review, West Branch,* and elsewhere.

Originally from Detroit, TOMMYE BLOUNT is the author of the poetry collection *Fantasia for the Man in Blue* (Four Way, 2020), which was a finalist for the National Book Award, the Kate Tufts Discovery Award, the Lambda Literary Award in Gay Poetry, and the Hurston/Wright Legacy Award. The recipient of awards and fellowships from Bread Loaf, Cave Canem, Kresge Arts, and the Whiting Foundation, he lives in Novi, Michigan.

CYNTHIA BOERSMA was born on a submarine base in New London, Connecticut, and for an embarrassingly long time thought this meant she had been born underwater. She currently practices as a psychotherapist after decades working as a civil rights lawyer. Her poems have appeared in *American Journal of Poetry* and *The Laurel Review*. She lives in the mountains of Southern Oregon.

TRACI BRIMHALL is the current poet laureate of Kansas, where she teaches at Kansas State University. She is the author of four collections of poetry, most recently *Come the Slumbers to the Land of Nod* (Copper Canyon, 2020).

Born in Atlanta, Georgia, GEOFFREY BROCK is the author of several poetry collections—most recently *After*, which is forthcoming in 2024 from Paul Dry Books. His many translations from Italian include Giuseppe Ungaretti's *Allegria* (Arechipelago, 2020), which won the National Translation Award. He teaches at the University of Arkansas.

JAMES BRUNTON is the author of *Opera on TV* (The Operating System, 2019) and co-author, with Russell Evatt, of the chapbook *The Future Is a Faint Song* (Dream Horse, 2014). His work appears in *The Cincinnati Review, Denver Quarterly, The Journal,* and elsewhere. He teaches at the University of Nebraska.

JOSEPH J. CAPISTA is the author of *Intrusive Beauty* (Ohio UP, 2019). His poems have appeared in *Agni, The Hudson Review, Ploughshares,* and on *Poetry Daily*. The recipient of awards from the National Endowment for the Humanities, the Maryland State Arts Council, Sewanee, and Bread Loaf, he teaches at Towson University and lives with his family in Baltimore.

STEPHANIE CHOI's poems appear in *Bellevue Literary Review, Blackbird, New Ohio Review, Pank,* and elsewhere. She is currently the poet-in-residence at Sewanee: The University of the South. Her debut collection, *The Lengest Neoi,* was selected by Brenda Shaughnessy for the 2023 Iowa Poetry Prize and will be published by the University of Iowa Press in 2024.

EMILY CINQUEMANI's poetry appears in *Colorado Review, Ploughshares, Southern Indiana Review, 32 Poems,* and elsewhere. She teaches at The South Carolina Governor's School for the Arts and Humanities.

KATIE CONDON teaches at Southern Methodist University. Her poems appear in *The American Poetry Review, The New Yorker, Ploughshares,* and elsewhere. She is the author of *Praying Naked* (Ohio State, 2020), winner of the Charles B. Wheeler Poetry Prize.

ANDREW COLLARD is the author of *Sprawl* (Ohio UP, 2023), winner of the Hollis Summers Poetry Prize. His poems appear in *Agni, Best New Poets, Ploughshares,* and elsewhere. He currently lives in Grand Rapids, Michigan, with his son and teaches at Grand Valley State University.

REBECCA ENTEL mentors through the PEN America Prison and Justice Writing program. She is the author of a novel, *Fingerprints of Previous Owners* (The Unnamed, 2017), and her short prose appears in *Cleaver, Guernica, Jellyfish Review, Literary Hub,* and elsewhere. She teaches at Cornell College, where she directs the Center for the Literary Arts.

CHRIS FORHAN has published three poetry collections and two books of nonfiction, most recently *A Mind Full of Music: Essays on Imagination and Popular Song* (Overcup, 2022). He has won three Pushcart Prizes and an NEA Fellowship. He teaches at Butler University.

Originally from Albuquerque, New Mexico, MATTHEW LAWRENCE GARCIA lives in Düsseldorf, Germany, where he teaches at Heinrich Heine University. He holds an MA from University College London and was a Fulbright Scholar. His fiction appears in *Gulf Coast* and *The Santa Monica Review* and was a two-time finalist for the *American Short Fiction* Halifax Ranch Prize and the *Southwest Review* David Meyerson Prize. His literature podcast is *Doggerel Diaries.*

MARK HALLIDAY is the author of seven poetry collections, most recently *Losers Dream On* (U of Chicago, 2018). His awards include the Rome Prize from the American Academy of Arts and Letters. He teaches at Ohio University.

MYRONN HARDY's most recent poetry collection is *Aurora Americana* (Princeton, 2023). His poems appear in *The Georgia Review*, *The New York Times Magazine*, *Ploughshares*, *Poetry*, and elsewhere. He lives in Maine.

Poems by DANA ISOKAWA appear in *The American Poetry Review* and *Narrative*. She is a contributing editor of *Poets & Writers* and editor-in-chief of *The Margins*, the literary magazine of the Asian American Writers' Workshop.

JAMES JABAR is the author of the chapbook *Whatever Happened to Black Boys?* (Texas Review, 2020), and his poems appear in *The Freshwater Review*, *The Minnesota Review*, and *Southern Cultures*. He teaches at Guilford Technical Community College. When Jabar is not writing poetry or mentoring students, he reviews music and movies on YouTube under the pseudonym Kakashi Cowboy.

CHRISTEN NOEL KAUFFMAN's debut collection *The Science of Things We Can Believe* won the 2023 Ghost Peach Press Prize in Poetry and is forthcoming. Her chapbook *Notes to a Mother God* was published by Paper Nautilus in 2021, and her work can be found in *The Cincinnati Review*, *Tupelo Quarterly*, *Smokelong Quarterly*, and *A Harp in the Stars: An Anthology of Lyric Essays*.

DAVID KEPLINGER is the author of eight collections of poetry, most recently *Ice* (Milkweed, 2023), and his awards include the 2019 UNT Rilke Prize. He has translated Jan Wagner's *The Art of the Topiary* (Milkweed, 2017) and Carsten René Nielsen's *Forty-One Objects* (Bitter Oleander, 2019), which was a finalist for the National Translation Award. He teaches at American University.

KIM HYESOON has published over a dozen poetry collection in Korean; her most recent US publication is *Phantom Pain Wings* (New Directions, 2023, translated by Don Mee Choi). Her international honors include the Griffin Poetry Prize, the Cikada Prize, and the Daesan Literary Award. She lives in Seoul. For more information, see page 153.

CINDY KING is the author of *Zoonotic* (Tinderbox, 2022), and *Lesser Birds of Paradise* (Louisana Literature, 2022). Her poems appear in *The Cincinnati Review*, *The Sun*, *Threepenny Review*, and elsewhere. She teaches at Utah Tech University and is on the editorial staffs of *Route 7 Review*, *The Southern Quill*, and *Seneca Review*.

A poet and essayist, MELISSA KWASNY has published seven poetry collections including *Where Outside the Body Is the Soul Today* (U of Washington, 2017) and *The Cloud Path*, which is forthcoming from Milkweed Editions. Her nonfiction book *Putting on the Dog: The Animal Origins of What We Wear* was published by Trinity University Press in 2022. Kwasny was appointed poet laureate of Montana in 2019.

VIVIAN LAMARQUE, born in 1946, is one of the most acclaimed Italian poets writing today. Over the course of a dozen books—from *Teresino*, which won the Premio Viareggio for best first collection in 1981, to her most recent volume, *L'amore da vecchia*, which came out in 2022—she has transformed the raw materials of her unusual biography into a singular body of work. For more information, see page 15.

REBECCA LINDENBERG is the author of three poetry collections, including *The Logan Notebooks* (Mountain West Poetry Series, 2014) and *Our Splendid Failure to Do the Impossible*, which is forthcoming from BOA Editions in 2024. She teaches at University of Cincinnati and serves as poetry editor of *The Cincinnati Review*.

TIMOTHY LIU's latest book of poems is *Down Low and Lowdown: Bedside Bottom-Feeder Blues* (Barrow Street, 2023). Sone of his new poems appear in *Fence*, *Michigan Quarterly Review*, and *Poetry*. A reader of occult esoterica, Liu lives in the Hudson Valley and teaches at SUNY New Paltz and Vassar College.

MAJA LUKIC just received her MFA in poetry from Warren Wilson College. Her work appears in *The Adroit Journal, Colorado Review, Narrative, A Public Space,* and elsewhere. She lives in Brooklyn, New York.

Born in Benghazi, Libya, KHALED MATTAWA has received a MacArthur Foundation Fellowship, an Academy of American Poets Award, the PEN Award for Poetry in Translation, and more. His latest book of poems is *Fugitive Atlas* (Graywolf, 2020). He is the editor-in-chief of *Michigan Quarterly Review* and teaches at the University of Michigan.

JENNIFER MILITELLO is the author of *Knock Wood* (Dzanc, 2019), winner of the Dzanc Nonfiction Prize, and the poetry collection *The Pact* (Tupelo, 2021), as well as four previous collections of poetry. Her work appears in *Best American Poetry, The Nation, The New Republic, The Paris Review,* and elsewhere. She teaches at New England College.

Born in Charlotte, North Carolina, RANDY F. NELSON is the author of the short fiction collection *The Imaginary Lives of Mechanical Men* (U of Georgia, 2006), which won the Flannery O'Connor Award. His individual stories have also been recognized in *Pushcart Prize XXXII, Best American Short Stories* and elsewhere. His latest book is a mystery titled *A Duplicate Daughter* (Harvard Square, 2017).

MATTHEW NIENOW is the author of *If Nothing*, which is forthcoming from Alice James Books in 2025, and *House of Water* (2016). His work has appeared in *Gulf Coast, New England Review, Ploughshares, Poetry* and elsewhere. He has received fellowships from the Poetry Foundation and the National Endowment for the Arts. He lives in Port Townsend, Washington, with his wife and two sons and works as a mental health counselor.

CINDY JUYOUNG OK's debut poetry collection *Ward Toward* won the 2023 Yale Younger Poets Prize and was published by Yale University Press in 2024. Her poems appear in *The Kenyon Review, The Nation, New England Review, Poetry*, and elsewhere, and her translations appear in *Asymptote* and *The Hopkins Review*. She lives in Berkeley, California.

CAROLYN OROSZ lives in Vermont and reads for *The New England Review*. Her work appears in *Gulf Coast, The Journal, Poetry Northwest, Southeast Review*, and elsewhere.

LAMA ROD OWENS is a Black Buddhist Southern Queen with a Master of Divinity degree from Harvard Divinity School. He is the author of the bestsellers *The New Saints: From Broken Hearts to Spiritual Warriors* (Sounds True, 2023) and *Love and Rage: The Path of Liberation through Anger* (North Atlantic, 2020), and co-author of *Radical Dharma: Talking Race, Love and Liberation* (2016). He lives in Atlanta, Georgia.

JAMES CONOR PATTERSON is a writer from the north of Ireland. His debut poetry collection *bandit country* (Picador, 2022) received an Eric Gregory Award in 2019 and was shortlisted for the T. S. Eliot Prize, the John Pollard Poetry Prize, and the Michael Murphy Memorial Prize. He also edited an anthology of Irish border writing entitled *The New Frontier: Reflections from the Irish Border*, which was published by New Island Books in 2021.

ISAAC PICKELL is a Black and Jewish poet & PhD Candidate who lives in Detroit, Michigan. He is the author of *It's not over once you figure it out* (Black Ocean, 2023) and *everything saved will be last* (2021). His recent work appears in *Denver Quarterly, Passages North, Poetry Daily, Swamp Pink*, and elsewhere.

Work by CAROL QUINN appears in *American Literary Review, The Emily Dickinson Review, Pleiades, Poetry Daily*, and elsewhere. Her first book of poems, *Acetylene* (Cider Press, 2010), won the Cider Press Review Book Award. She teaches in the English Department at Towson University and at a school for neurodiverse learners. With her fiancé, she raises corn, tomatoes, cats, chickens, and goats.

CAMILLE RANKINE is the daughter of Jamaican immigrants. Her first book of poetry, *Incorrect Merciful Impulses,* was published in 2016 by Copper Canyon Press, and her chapbook, *Slow Dance with Trip Wire*, was selected by Cornelius Eady for the Poetry Society of America's 2010 New York Chapbook Fellowship. She has received fellowships from The MacDowell Colony, the Bread Loaf Writers' Conference, and the National Endowment for the Arts, and her poetry appears in *The New Yorker, The New York Times, Poetry, A Public Space, Tin House*, and elsewhere. She co-chairs the Brooklyn Book Festival Literary Council and teaches at Carnegie Mellon University.

TYLER RASO is a poet, teacher, and multimedia artist. Their work appears in *Black Warrior Review, The Journal, Poetry, Split Lip Magazine*, and elsewhere. They are the author of the chapbook *In my dreams/I love like an idea*, which won the 2022 Frontier Digital Chapbook Contest. They feel most at home near rivers.

PAISLEY REKDAL is the author of four books of nonfiction and seven books of poetry, including *Nightingale* (Copper Canyon, 2019), *Appropriate: A Provocation* (Norton, 2021), and, most recently, *West: A Translation* (Copper Canyon, 2023). She is the editor and creator of the digital archive projects *West, Mapping Literary Utah*, and *Mapping Salt Lake City*. Her work has received the Amy Lowell Poetry Traveling Fellowship, a Guggenheim Fellowship, an NEA Fellowship, Pushcart Prizes, the Academy of American Poets Laureate Fellowship, a Fulbright Fellowship, and various state arts council awards. The former Utah poet laureate, she teaches at the University of Utah where she directs the American West Center.

CINTIA SANTANA teaches fiction and poetry workshops in Spanish, as well as literary translation courses at Stanford University. Her work appears in *Best New Poets 2020*, the 2023 *Best of the Net Anthology*, and in the Academy of American Poets' *Poem-a-Day* series. Her debut *The Disordered Alphabet* was published by Four Way Books in 2023 and shortlisted for the 2023 Golden Poppy Award in Poetry.

Work by HASANTHIKA SIRISENA has appeared recently in *Electric Literature*, *The Georgia Review*, and *Literary Hub*, and has been named notable by *Best American Short Stories* and *Best American Essays*. They're currently on faculty at the Vermont College of Fine Arts and Susquehanna University, and on the editorial board at Great Circle Books. Their short story collection *The Other One* (Massachusetts, 2016) won the Juniper Prize, and their essay collection *Dark Tourist* (Mad Creek, 2022) won the Gournay Prize.

Born and raised in Philadelphia, ALLYSON STACK teaches at the University of Edinburgh. Her short stories have appeared in print and electronic journals throughout the United States, Britain, and Ireland. Her novel *Under the Heartless Blue* was published by Freight Books in 2016, and she is currently working on a book about Edith Wharton.

CHARLES STEPHENS is based in Atlanta. His work appears in *Isele*, *The Lumiere Review*, *Queerlings*, and the anthology *For Colored Boys Who Have Considered Suicide When the Rainbow Is Still Not Enough*. He was a 2023 Periplus Fellow and a 2023 Roots Wounds Words Words of Resistance & Restoration Fellow. His writing has been supported by *Tin House*, Hurston/Wright, and the Lambda Literary Writer's Retreat for Emerging LGBTQ Voices.

RHETT ISEMAN TRULL's poetry collection, *The Real Warnings* (Anhinga, 2009), won the Devil's Kitchen Reading Award, the Brockman Campbell Book Award, and the Oscar Arnold Young Award. Her poetry appears in *The American Poetry Review*, *Image*, *The National Poetry Review*, *Sugar House Review*, and elsewhere. She edits *Cave Wall* and serves as president of The Nina Riggs Poetry Foundation.

German poet, essayist, and translator JAN WAGNER was born in Hamburg and currently lives in Berlin. He is the author of seven poetry collections for which he has received the Georg-Büchner-Prize, among other prominent awards. His English selections include *Self-Portrait with a Swarm of Bees* translated by Iain Galbraith (Arc UK, 2015), and *The Art of Topiary* translated by David Keplinger (Milkweed, 2017). For more information, see page 119.

LAURA PAUL WATSON lives in Pine, Colorado. She was recently shortlisted for the Manchester Poetry Prize, and her work appears in *Agni, Beloit Poetry Journal, Boulevard, Poetry*, and elsewhere.

Born near Basra, Iraq, SAADI YOUSSEF (1934-2021) is considered one of the most important contemporary poets in the Arab world. Following his experience as a political prisoner in Iraq, he spent most of his life in exile, working as a teacher and literary journalist throughout North Africa and the Middle East. He published over forty books of poetry, two novels, a book of short stories, and several books of nonfiction. Youssef, who spent the last two decades of his life in London, translated into Arabic works by Walt Whitman, Ngugi wa Thiongo, Federico Garcia Lorca, and many others. For more information, see page 43.

Required Reading

(issue 38)

(For each issue, we ask that our contributors recommend up to three recent titles. What follows is the list generated by the writers in issue 38.)

Jason Allen-Paisant, *Self-Portrait as Othello* (Rebecca Lindenberg)

Stephen Armstrong, *I Want You Around: The Ramones and the Making of Rock 'n' Roll High School* (Cindy King)

Jubi Arriola-Headley, *original kink* (Charles Stephens)

Sarah Bakewell, *Humanly Possible: Seven Hundred Years of Humanist Freethinking, Inquiry, and Hope* (Dana Isokawa)

Jesse Ball, *Autoportrait* (Xavier Blackwell-Lipkind)

Taneum Bambrick, *Intimacies, Received* (Diannely Antigua)

Gary J. Bass, *Judgment at Tokyo: World War II on Trial and the Making of Modern Asia* (Randy F. Nelson)

Claire Bateman, *Wonders of the Invisible World* (Mark Halliday)

Gabrielle Bates, *Judas Goat* (Allison Adair, Traci Brimhall)

Oliver Baez Bendorf, *Advantages of Being Evergreen* (James Brunton)

Ana Božičević, *New Life* (Timothy Liu)

Anna Burns, *Milkman* (Allyson Stack)

Taylor Byas, *I Done Clicked My Heels Three Times* (Rebecca Lindenberg)

Ina Cariño, *Feast* (James Jabar)

Catherine Cezina Choy, *Asian American Histories of the United States* (Rick Barot)

Sandra Cisneros, *Woman Without Shame* (Jan Beatty)

John Lee Clark, *How to Communicate* (Tommye Blount)

Brian Cochran, *Translation Zone* (Cintia Santana)

Andrew Cohen, *The Sorrow Apartments* (Geoffrey Brock)

Kathryn Cowles, *Maps and Transcripts of the Ordinary World* (Rebecca Lindenberg)

Morri Creech, *The Sentence* (Chris Forhan)

Adam Deutsch, *Every Transmission* (James Brunton)

Alisha Dietzman, *Sweet Movie* (Carolyn Orosz)

Tishani Doshi, *A God at the Door* (Allison Adair)

Jehanne Dubrow, *Exhibitions: Essays on Art and Atrocity* (Hasanthika Sirisena)

Rikki Ducornet, *Trafik* (Matthew Nienow)

Patricia Duncker, *Hallucinating Foucault* (Allyson Stack)

Debra Magpie Earling, *The Lost Journals of Sacajawea* (Melissa Kwasny)

Jennifer Egan, *The Candy House* (Emily Cinquemani)

Anne Enright, *The Wren, the Wren* (Carol Quinn)

Mariana Enríquez, *The Dangers of Smoking in Bed*, trans. Megan McDowell (Anthony M. Abboreno)

Mariana Enríquez, *Our Share of Night*, trans. Megan McDowell (Mya Matteo Alexice)

Katie Farris, *Standing in the Forest of Being Alive* (Emily Cinquemani)

Camonghne Felix, *Dyscalculia: A Love Story of Epic Miscalculation* (Diannely Antigua)

Megan Fernandes, *I Do Everything I'm Told* (Tyler Raso)

Nicole Flattery, *Nothing Special* (James Conor Patterson)

Sidik Fofana, *Stories from the Tenants Downstairs* (Matthew Lawrence Garcia)

Graham Foust, *Terminations* (Timothy Liu)

Hafizah Augustus Geter, *The Black Period* (Camille Rankine)

Chantal Gibson, *How She Read* (Tommye Blount)

Renee Gladman, *Plans for Sentences* (Cindy Juyoung Ok)

Louise Glück, *Marigold and Rose* (Cynthia Boersma)

Louise Glück, *Winter Recipes from the Collective* (Melissa Kwasny)

Jennifer Grotz, *Still Falling* (Geoffrey Brock, Katie Condon)

Yaa Gyasi, *Transcendent Kingdom* (Matthew Lawrence Garcia)

Shahnaz Habib, *Airplane Mode: An Irreverent History of Travel* (Hasanthika Sirisena)

Leslie Harrison, *Reck* (Joseph J. Capista)

Terrance Hayes, *So to Speak* (Cindy King)

Destiny Hemphill, *Motherworld: A Devotional for the After-Life* (James Jabar)

Tricia Hersey, *Rest Is Resistance: A Manifesto* (Lama Rod Owens)

Noor Hindi, *Dear God. Dear Bones. Dear Yellow.* (Tyler Raso)

Dennis Hinrichsen, *Flesh-plastique* (Andrew Collard)

Tony Hoagland, *Turn Up the Ocean* (Joseph J. Capista, Mark Halliday)

Kazuo Ishiguro, *Kiara and the Sun* (Cynthia Boersma)

K. Iver, *Short Film Starring My Beloved's Red Bronco* (Traci Brimhall, Christen Noel Kauffman)

Max Jacob, *The Dice Cup*, trans. Ian Seed (David Keplinger)

A. Van Jordan, *When I Waked I Cried to Dream Again* (James Jabar)

Kasey Jueds, *The Thicket* (Rhett Iseman Trull)

Laura Kasischke, *Lightning Falls in Love* (Chris Forhan)

Louise Kennedy, *Trespasses* (Matthew Nienow)

Saba Keramati, *Self-Mythology* (Stephanie Choi)

Sorayya Khan, *We Take Our Cities with Us* (Hasanthika Sirisena)

Kim Hyesoon, *Phantom Pain Wings*, trans. Don Mee Choi (Jennifer Militello)

Etheridge Knight, *The Lost Etheridge: Uncollected Poems of Etheridge Knight* (Jan Beatty)

Talia Lakshmi Kolluri, *What We Fed to the Manticore* (Dana Isokawa)

R. F. Kuang, *Babel: Or the Necessity of Violence: An Arcane History of the Oxford Translators' Revolution* (Mya Matteo Alexice)

Eugenia Leigh, *Bianca* (Allison Adair, Diannely Antigua, Traci Brimhall)

Andrew Leland, *The Country of the Blind: A Memoir at the End of Sight* (Randy F. Nelson)

Anni Liu, *Border Vista* (Katie Condon)

James Longenbach, *Forever* (Joseph J. Capista)

Michael Longley, *The Slain Birds* (Cynthia Boersma)

Emily Lee Luan, *Return* (Jan Beatty, Carolyn Orosz)

Valeria Luiselli, Ed., *The Best Short Stories 2022: The O. Henry Prize Winners* (Jennifer Militello)

Douglas Manuel, *Trouble Funk* (Chris Forhan, Charles Stephens)

Shena McAuliffe, *We Are a Teeming Wilderness* (Rebecca Entel)

Elizabeth McCracken, *The Hero of This Book* (Rebecca Entel)

Erika Meitner, *Useful Junk* (Katie Condon)

Clyo Mendoza, *Silencio* (Cintia Santana)

Steven Millhauser, *Disruptions* (Randy F. Nelson)

Maggie Milner, *Couplets: A Love Story* (Camille Rankine)

Katherine Min, *The Fetishist* (Geoffrey Brock)

Jenny Molberg, *The Court of No Record* (David Keplinger)

Tamsyn Muir, The Locked Tomb Series (Rhett Iseman Trull)

Abigail Parry, *I Think We're Alone Now* (Paisley Rekdal)

Craig Santos Perez, *from unincorporated territory [åmot]* (Rick Barot)

Kevin Prufer, *The Art of Fiction* (Carol Quinn)

Yung Pueblo, *Lighter: Let Go of the Past, Connect with the Present, Expand the Future* (Lama Rod Owens)

Hugh Raffles, *The Book of Uncomformities: Speculations on Lost Time* (Cintia Santana)

Srikanth Reddy, *Underworld Lit* (Jennifer Militello)

Roger Reeves, *Best Barbarian* (Cindy Juyoung Ok)

Padraig Regan, *Some Integrity* (James Conor Patterson)

Vincent Antonio Rendoni, *A Grito Contest in the Afterlife* (Matthew Lawrence Garcia)

Monica Rico, *Pinion* (Andrew Collard)

Cole Arthur Riley, *Black Liturgies: Prayers, Poems, and Meditations for Staying Human* (Lama Rod Owens)

Iliana Rocha, *The Many Deaths of Inocencio Rodriguez* (Andrew Collard)

Mary Ruefle, *The Book* (Cindy King)

Leslie Sainz, *Have You Been Long Enough at Table* (Carolyn Orosz)

Claudio Saunt, *Unworthy Republic: The Dispossession of Native Americans and the Road to Indian Territory* (Paisley Rekdal)

Robyn Schiff, *Information Desk: An Epic* (Tommye Blount)

Christina Sharpe, *Ordinary Notes* (Rick Barot, Rebecca Entel, Isaac Pickell)

Charles Simic, *No Land in Sight* (David Keplinger)

Ali Smith, *Companion Piece* (Melissa Kwasny)

Zadie Smith, *Intimations* (Myronn Hardy)

Julia Ridley Smith, *Sum of Trifles* (Emily Cinquemani)

Jess Tanck, *Winter Here* (Stephanie Choi)

Mosab Abu Toha, *Things You May Find Hidden in My Ear: Poems from Gaza* (Camille Rankine)

Brian K. Vaughn, The *Saga* Series (Rhett Iseman Trull)

Jan Wagner, *The Art of Topiary*, trans. David Keplinger (Laura Paul Watson)

Sara Moore Wagner, *Hillbilly Madonna* (Christen Noel Kauffman)

Sara Moore Wagner, *Swan Wife* (Christen Noel Kauffman)

Aimée Walsh, *Exile* (James Conor Patterson)

Alan Warner, *The Deadman's Pedal* (Allyson Stack)

Bryan Washington, *Family Meal* (Charles Stephens)

Lindsey Webb, *Plat* (Stephanie Choi)

Simon West, *Prickly Moses* (Myronn Hardy)

Joy Williams, *Harrow* (Paisley Rekdal)

Jane Wong, *How to Not Be Afraid of Everything* (Tyler Raso)

Jane Wong, *Meet Me Tonight in Atlantic City* (Matthew Nienow)

Jade Yeung, *Anti* (Mya Matteo Alexice)

Javier Zamora, *Solito* (Myronn Hardy, Carol Quinn)

The Copper Nickel Editors' Prizes

(est. 2015)

(Two $500 prizes are awarded to the "most exciting work" published
in each issue, as determined by a vote of the *Copper Nickel* staff)

Past Winners

fall 2023 (issue 37)

Owen McLeod, poetry
Becky Hagenston, prose

spring 2023 (issue 36)

Rita Mookerjee, poetry
Julia Ridley Smith, prose

fall 2022 (issue 35)

Ariana Benson, poetry
Molly Beckwith, prose

spring 2022 (issue 34)

Indrani Sengupta, poetry
Alyssa Quinn, prose

fall 2021 (issue 33)

Natlie Tombasco, poetry
Dan Leach, prose

fall 2020 (issue 31&2)

Michael Bazzett, poetry
Matt Donovan, poetry
Aidan Forster, prose
Kathy Fish, prose

spring 2020 (issue 30)

Andrea Cohen, poetry
Maureen Langloss, prose

fall 2019 (issue 29)

Derek Robbins, poetry
Sam Simas, prose

spring 2019 (issue 28)

Catherine Pierce, poetry
Sarah Anne Strickley, prose

fall 2018 (issue 27)

Jenny Boychuk, poetry
Farah Ali, prose

spring 2018 (issue 26)

Cindy Tran, poetry
Gianni Skaragas, prose

fall 2017 (issue 25)

Sarah Carson, poetry
Meagan Ciesla, prose

spring 2017 (issue 24)

Ashley Keyser, poetry
Robert Long Foreman, prose

fall 2016 (issue 23)

Tim Carter, poetry
Evelyn Somers, prose

spring 2016 (issue 22)

Bernard Farai Matambo, poetry
Sequoia Nagamatsu, prose

subscription rates

For regular folks:

one year (two issues)—$24
two years (four issues)—$42
five years (ten issues)—$80

For student folks:

one year (two issues)—$20
two years (four issues)—$36
five years (ten issues)—$65

For more information, visit: www.copper-nickel.org

To go directly to subscriptions
visit: coppernickel.submittable.com

To order back issues, email wayne.miller@ucdenver.edu